THE SECRET OF THE MIRRORS

So many things about Fell Andred had bothered Janie, so many little things didn't seem to fit—disjointed fragments of thought rushed past her. The night they'd made the amulet, when they had found that no mirror could be moved from the house. The night she had gone through the double mirrors to rescue the others from Aric. The fight with Elwyn—

Oh, it was no good! With a sharp sound of frustration she shook her head, wishing wildly, illogically, that she were a sorceress like Thia Pendriel. Morgana was somewhere in the castle, Janie felt sure of that, and if they could only work the proper spell they could simply look through the mirrors and find her. That is, they could find her as long as . . .

A long wondering breath escaped Janie's lips, and as the full moon separated itself from the hill it shone upon her transfigured face. That was it. That was the answer.

Alys was at the door, gasoline can in hand.

"Alys, Charles, put those down, you're not going to need them."

"What?"

"I know where Morgana is."

ALSO BY L.J. SMITH

THE VAMPIRE DIARIES

Volume I: *The Awakening*
Volume II: *The Struggle*
Volume III: *The Fury*
Volume IV: *Dark Reunion*

THE SECRET CIRCLE TRILOGY

Volume I: *The Initiation*
Volume II: *The Captive*
Volume III: *The Power*

AVAILABLE FROM HARPERPAPERBACKS

THE *Night* OF

THE *Solstice*

L.J. SMITH

HarperPaperbacks
A Division of HarperCollinsPublishers

HarperPaperbacks *A Division of* HarperCollins*Publishers*
10 East 53rd Street, New York, N.Y. 10022

Copyright © 1987 by Lisa Smith
All rights reserved. No part of this book may be used or
reproduced in any manner whatsoever without written
permission of the publisher, except in the case of brief
quotations embodied in critical articles and reviews. For
information address HarperCollins*Publishers*,
10 East 53rd Street, New York, N.Y. 10022.

A previous edition of this book was published in 1987 by
Macmillan Publishing Company. This edition is
published by arrangement with Macmillan Publishing
Company.

Cover illustration by Danilo Ducak

First HarperPaperbacks printing: September 1993

Printed in the United States of America

HarperPaperbacks and colophon are
trademarks of HarperCollins*Publishers*

10 9 8 7 6 5 4 3 2 1

This book is for Julie, without whose insightful criticism, stubborn optimism, and all-around heroism it would never have been written.

CONTENTS

chapter 1

THE VIXEN

The vixen was waiting.

Dappled sunlight fell around her onto the soft dirt beneath the orange trees, gilding her russet fur and striking an occasional brief gleam from her yellow eyes. She had waited here in the orchard since dawn and she was prepared to go on waiting until moonset if necessary. She required only one child, but that child must be alone, and there must be no other human on the street to bear witness.

She was very tired.

At last the front door of the house across the street opened. A ripple of tension went through the vixen's body, starting at the tip of her tail and racing upward to set her sensitive whiskers aquiver. Her silken ears strained forward as a figure emerged from the house.

It was the young one, the smallest one. And she was alone.

The vixen's teeth clicked together gently.

Claudia was on her way to the mailbox. It was a cool Saturday morning in December; her father was reading the newspaper, her·mother was in the darkroom, Alys was playing tennis, Charles was still in bed, and Janie was—well, Janie was doing whatever it was Janie did. So Claudia, who always had free time, had been delegated to get the mail.

She never saw the animal until it was upon her.

It happened all at once, just as she was taking two handfuls of letters out of the box. It happened so quickly that she had no time to scream or even to be frightened. With one smooth motion the animal sprang at her, and she felt the brush of hard teeth against her knuckles, and then it was past her.

Claudia sat down hard and unexpectedly, biting her tongue. The pain of this brought tears to her eyes as she looked at the creature which had frightened her.

It was a fox, or at least it looked like the foxes she had seen at the exhibit in Irvine Park. A fox had jumped on her. Claudia's first impulses were to run into the house and tell someone about it and to cry.

Two things stopped her. The first was that the fox was beautiful. Its glossy fur was red as fire and its eyes were like golden jewels. Its slim body looked lithe and strong and very, very competent. The wildness of it took her breath away.

The second thing was that the fox was trotting off with one of her letters in its mouth.

Claudia's mouth opened and shut. She looked around the street for someone with whom to share this extraordinary sight, but there was no one. When she looked back at the fox, it had stopped and was facing her again, watching her with its golden eyes. When it saw it had her attention, it turned and walked a few steps away, looking over its shoulder.

Slowly, Claudia got up. She took a step toward the fox.

The fox took two steps away.

Claudia stopped.

The fox stopped.

"Hey," said Claudia. She couldn't think of anything else to say. "Hey," she said again.

The fox dropped the letter and looked at her, panting gently.

This time it let her get within arm's reach before it moved, and then it nipped the letter from the ground and scampered down the road.

But always it looked over its shoulder, as if to make sure she was coming.

It led her down Taft Avenue and up Center Street. It led her past the orange grove, past the quiet houses, and past the vacant lot, until it came to the hill. And then it disappeared.

There were no cross streets here, only a tall iron gate. Behind the gate was a gravel road which led up to a huge old house. Claudia hesitated, standing first on one foot, then on the other. Children weren't allowed to go near the old house on the hill, not even on Halloween. Strange stories were told about the woman who lived there.

But the fox had Claudia's letter, and the fox was beautiful.

Claudia squeezed between the bars of the gate.

The gravel road was long and steep as it climbed the hill. Tall trees overhung it, and Claudia had the odd feeling as she walked that the trees were closing in behind her, cutting her off from the rest of Villa Park.

Rising above the trees at the top of the hill was the house, with its massive walls of gray stone and its four tall turrets. Claudia slipped through another gate. In the distance she caught a glimpse of red, and she followed it all the way around the towering house to the back. And there was the fox, caught between Claudia and a huge wooden door. If it ran, she thought, it would have to run toward her.

But, as Claudia hurried forward to trap it, the fox darted through the half-open door into the house.

Claudia clapped her hand to her mouth. Then she crept to the door and peeked inside.

The house was dark and still. When her eyes had adjusted to the dimness she saw the fox sitting in the middle of an enormous room looking at her, the letter between its front paws.

A tingling feeling started between Claudia's shoulder blades and spread down to her palms and up her neck. Sunlight and open air were right behind her, and for a moment she thought she would just run back down the road to Center Street.

Instead she put one foot inside the doorway.

The tingling feeling grew stronger. Outside, the wind seemed to hold its breath. Inside, the house was empty and echoing, and the air was cool.

Claudia looked at the fox and the fox looked at Claudia. And then Claudia took another step and both her feet were inside the house.

"Right!" said the fox. "Now stay in!"

chapter 2

THE SUMMONS

There were four children in the Hodges-Bradley household. Their mother, who had been Dr. Eileen Bradley before she married, and their father, who had been Mr. Michael Hodges, had planned it this way. They'd decided to have a nice big family so that no child of theirs would ever be lonely for lack of a brother or sister as a playmate. Consequently they were a little disappointed when their children, though generally cheerful and obliging, showed no inclination whatsoever to play together. It wasn't that the children disliked each other; there was simply too much difference in their ages and interests.

Claudia thought about this as she slowly walked home from the house on the hill, a very damp and crumpled letter clutched in her hand. She thought about it because her brother and sisters had suddenly become terribly important to her. And the reason they had become important was that the fox wanted them.

No, not fox, she corrected herself. Vixen. That was what the animal had called herself when Claudia asked. "I am a vixen, a female fox," she had replied with a quiver of her nostrils, and Claudia had immediately recognized that a vixen was a very grand and glorious thing to be.

"I want you to come back here," the vixen had said, "sometime after sunset. Say, as near to seven o'clock as you can manage. And I want you to bring your brother and sisters. Can you do it?"

And Claudia had said she could do it. She had given her word. And now she was faced with the problem of *how* to do it, how to explain to the others, who were old enough to be skeptical about magic, so they would understand.

Alys was the oldest. She was tall and fair-haired and graceful. This year she had started high school and she was captain of a girls' soccer team called the Blue Demons, and vice-president of her class. Alys was kind to Claudia, but she was the sort of girl adults called "practical" and "responsible." Alys, thought Claudia, did not believe in magic.

You could tell at a glance that Charles was Alys's younger brother. Charles could do almost everything, but he usually didn't. He called this being "laid-back." Charles rather thought he might be a famous artist someday, and in the meantime he drew a comic strip, Hugo the Hippopotamus, for the junior-high-school newspaper.

7

He liked science fiction. Science fiction, thought Claudia hopefully, was a little bit like magic.

Claudia herself wasn't talented, or a great athlete, or even tall. But her chunky little body was just right for rough-and-tumble sports and she never gave up. Sometimes Claudia's mother would ruffle her hair and say that Claudia was solid. Claudia wasn't exactly sure what she meant by this, but she liked the sound of it.

And then there was Janie. Nothing in the world seemed less likely, but Janie and Charles were twins. Janie was small and thin and dark and quiet, with tangled black hair which hung down her back. Her purple eyes looked at you as if they knew you and didn't like you much. When Janie had been Claudia's age some people at school had given her a test, and then they had called Janie's parents and told them that Janie was a genius, which everyone already knew anyway. Janie scorned magic.

Charles, Claudia decided, was the one most likely to believe her. She decided to tell him just as soon as her parents went out to dinner, and afterward they could tell the others together. But at six o'clock, just as Claudia was trying to get Charles away from Janie and the TV, Alys walked into the family room carrying an overnight bag.

"Where are you going?" gasped Claudia.

"To spend the night with my friend Geri Crowle," said Alys absently, rummaging about in the bag.

Claudia's throat constricted and her heart began to pound. Alys couldn't spend the night with her friend Geri Crowle.

"You can't go!" she said to Alys. "I mean—you can't go yet. I mean . . . Alys, I have something to tell you."

8

Alys blinked at her and the others looked up curiously. This wasn't how she'd wanted to do it, not facing all of them at once. But she had no choice.

"Something happened to me today," she said at last.

"Yes?" said Alys. She took a brush out of the bag and began to brush her hair.

Claudia decided to try another tack. "What do you think," she said carefully, "is the most wonderfulest, specialest, excitingest thing in the world?"

"A horse," said Alys.

"The Hope Diamond," said Janie.

"*Kryptonite?*" said Charles.

They laughed. Claudia stood very still, unsmiling.

"It's magic," she said, flatly. "And I've found it."

"Oh!" said Alys. She smiled suddenly, a nice smile. "What kind of magic?"

A great rushing warmth filled Claudia's chest. She had been just about dead certain that Alys wouldn't believe her. "It's a talking vixen," she said eagerly, leaning forward. "I was getting the mail this morning, and she took a letter from me. She talked to me. And she wants to meet *you*."

Alys's face changed. "Uh . . . sure, Claude, but you know I was just leaving. Maybe I could meet her tomorrow."

"But, Alys. She's in terrible trouble of some kind. She has to talk to all of us right away, tonight."

"Well, I'm kind of in a rush but . . . hey, isn't that her over there by the couch?"

Claudia looked. There was nothing by the couch.

"Uh, sure it is," said Charles, who was looking at Alys.

"Look, Claude, here's your friend. How's it going, Foxy Lady?" He smiled politely at empty air, and shook hands.

Suddenly Claudia understood. She felt hideously ashamed and hot tears flooded her eyes. "I'm not a liar!"

"Oh, bunny," said Alys. "It isn't lies. It's like when Charles makes up stories about Hugo. It shows you're creative."

Claudia began to cry. She didn't mean to. The lump in her throat rose up and swelled and blurred her vision. They didn't believe her, and they wouldn't come, and she'd promised the vixen. The vixen was waiting. She threw back her head and howled.

"Claudia!"

She went on crying. She ran into the corner and hid in the window seat. Between sobs she could hear Alys and Charles and Janie talking.

"Claudia . . . crying! Claudia never cries."

"Maybe she's having some sort of a mental breakdown."

"Janie, shut up! There's something wrong. Uh . . . Claude?" Alys's voice cut through Claudia's howling. "Who else was around when you met this magic vixen?"

"No-nobody," Claudia choked out. "I was alone with her in the old house on the hill."

Alys was shocked. "You know you're not supposed to go near there! What about the strange woman who lives in that house?"

"She wasn't home. I didn't see her."

"But you went inside?"

"The vixen t-t-took me!"

"Alys," said Charles, "somebody in that house is up to something."

"Fed her hallucinogenic drugs, maybe."

"You have such charming ideas, Janie," said Alys. Then she added, "Charles, this sounds a lot like some of your friends playing pranks to me."

"My friends? What about your friends? Who hung the Blue Demons banner from the top of the Villa Park clock tower? Who—"

"Whoever it is," Alys interrupted hastily, "they shouldn't be messing around with little kids. I mean, Claudia's only seven. It isn't right."

Charles's eyes gleamed with fun. "Maybe you ought to go over there and tell them that."

"Go *over* there? When I'm already late—"

"It's probably all in her head anyway," said Janie.

Alys, who had been leaning over to pick up her bag, suddenly stopped. She looked at Janie in annoyance. Then she looked sharply at Claudia, who looked back at her hopelessly, with her heart in her eyes.

There was a pause.

With a tremendous sigh, Alys let the bag thump to the floor.

"Okay, Claude," she said. "You can stop crying. You win. We're all going with you to see this magic vixen."

Charles and Janie put up an argument. Claudia hung on the fringe of the group, tears drying on her cheeks. She didn't care what they thought as long as they came.

At last Janie and Charles gave in.

"It might be dangerous," said Charles, hopefully.

Alys said seriously, "I'm going to take my baseball bat."

No one was happy with Claudia. By the time Alys had called Geri and they'd gotten the baseball bat and the flashlight, they had almost stopped believing anything was wrong.

"You sure this isn't a joke of *yours*, Claudia?"

Claudia shook her head dumbly.

They set out for the house on the hill.

chapter 3

THE STORY

With Claudia in the lead they walked around the side of the house to the heavy wooden back door.

Alys was holding the baseball bat in one hand and the flashlight in the other. "Knock," she said to Claudia.

"But she can't—"

"Just do it."

Claudia knocked. The door was hard and solid, and her knuckles made only a faint tapping sound.

No one answered.

"Ring the doorbell."

"There isn't one," said Charles.

"All right," said Alys, and she banged with the bat on the door. Claudia jumped at the sudden noise.

"That ought to wake 'em up," said Janie, and she chuckled.

"She's awake, but she can't open the door," said Claudia. "She's got *paws*."

Alys looked at her, then at the door. "Here, hold this," she said at last. She gave Claudia the flashlight and gently tried the door handle. "It isn't locked, anyway." Slowly she pushed the door open a few inches. Just like the door in any horror movie, it creaked. "I'll go in first. You hang on to the flashlight, Claudia."

Claudia was on Alys's heels as she pushed the door open and stepped inside. The flashlight threw a wavering ellipse of white on the floor and walls of the huge dark room. Charles crowded behind Claudia, breathing in her ear, and Janie shuffled in after him.

"We're here," Claudia called, but it was hard to call loudly into that silent darkness. "We're all inside," she piped again. The flashlight caught the gleam of a great chandelier overhead, and a mirror on the wall to the left, but the vixen was nowhere to be seen.

"Let's go," whispered Charles. "Nobody's home."

Just then, with a wrenching creak, the door slammed shut behind them. Charles yelled and grabbed the flashlight from Claudia, swinging it around toward the door. The pool of light fell squarely on Janie, one hand still on the doorknob. Janie giggled madly.

"You idiot!" said Alys, lowering the baseball bat. "I nearly brained you."

"Shhhh!" said Claudia. "I heard something. Over there."

Charles aimed the flashlight straight ahead. Yellow eyes leapt at them out of the dark, and then with a wriggle of motion the vixen was sitting on an overturned chair.

"All four of you," she said. "Good. I had feared—"

What she feared will never be known, for Alys, with a gasp, stumbled backward, running heavily into Charles. Charles yelled in pain and dropped the flashlight, which went dead on the floor. Janie began groping her way toward a light switch and accidentally poked Charles in the eye, and Charles yelled again.

"It's on the other side," came a voice from the darkness, a dry little voice which could only belong to the vixen. Janie fumbled across the door, making sweeping motions. Her hand caught on something and there was light.

The children turned as one to stare at the animal. They were all breathing hard.

"Enough nonsense," she said. "You are young enough to know better. Now, I have a very important matter to discuss with you, and I don't want any hitting"—to Alys —"or any shouting"—with a look at Charles—"or any pointless arguing"—with a significant glance in Janie's direction. "Is that understood? Then sit down and attend."

But only Claudia sat down, and no one else seemed to be paying much attention. Janie stood frozen. Charles wobbled back and forth drunkenly between the animal on the chair and the back door, while Alys made little charges at the vixen with the baseball bat.

"Stop that," said the vixen.

"You . . . yow . . . wow," said Alys. At least that was what it sounded like. She waved the baseball bat in rubbery circles around the vixen's head.

"Yes, I can talk, say it if you must and get it over with. I am even a—a witch's familiar, if you will. But I am not evil and I do not wish to see you hurt. On the contrary, I desperately need your help."

"Help . . . help . . . ," said Charles. Later he always insisted he'd only been repeating the vixen's words.

Meanwhile, Alys's frenzied gaze fell on Claudia, who was sitting only inches away from the vixen. With a gurgle, she flung herself between her small sister and the animal. Then she grabbed Claudia by the back of the collar, and brandishing the bat with the other hand began to drag her away.

"No," said Claudia. "Alys, no!" She fell flat on her stomach, clasping Alys around the ankles. "Alys, please!"

Alys merely tightened her grip. There was a look of fixed, mad determination in her eyes. With Claudia still attached she began to shuffle awkwardly backward toward the door, shaking the bat in the vixen's direction every few moments. There were books and knickknacks scattered on the floor; Claudia went sliding over each with a bump and a yelp. The vixen looked on in astonished scorn.

"Alys," whimpered Claudia, "Alys, stop." Alys collided with the door and fumbled for the knob, and Claudia reached the height of desperation.

"Alys," she said, and there was a new note in her voice, a note which made Alys look down into her small, commanding face. "Alys, *get a hold of yourself.*"

Something cleared in Alys's eyes, and she blinked; then her panting breath slowed and she stared down at Claudia. Claudia let go of Alys's ankles and sat up, rubbing her stomach. She looked at the vixen, then up at her sister.

"She doesn't want to hurt us, Alys," she said quietly. "She needs us."

Alys followed Claudia's gaze to the vixen, who soberly inclined her red-gold head.

A dazed and defeated expression came into Alys's eyes. Slowly she lowered the baseball bat until it dropped from her nerveless fingers to the ground. Then, casting one last glance about the room as if bidding good-bye to all hope of sanity, she knelt on the floor.

Charles rocked on his heels for a moment, and then, abruptly, he too sat down. But Janie was now walking round and round the vixen, looking at her from all angles.

"Holographic projection?" she mused.

"Sit down and shut up," replied the vixen coldly. "Oh, very well, touch me if you insist, but *quickly*. I have a long story to tell and a short time in which to tell it."

When Janie found the vixen solid she looked at her fingers for a moment as if they had betrayed her; then a slow, strange smile came to her face, the smile of someone who can't figure out how a magician does a trick, but who isn't going to be fooled anyway.

"Now sit!"

Janie sat.

"I have no more time for foolishness," said the vixen. "Listen carefully. You and your world are in terrible danger—"

"Huh? Our *world?*" said Charles.

"—because in just two weeks, on the night of the winter solstice, the mirrors will be open to all, and Cadal Forge can come through. And he *will* come through, too, unless Morgana can get here first and close him out."

"Morgana?" said Alys blankly.

"Morgana Shee is my mistress, and the lady of this house, and the greatest sorceress of her time. And she's been betrayed, captured, imprisoned, entrapped, and who knows what else! And it's up to us to save her because she's the only person who can close the mirrors! Well?" She swept them with a gaze from eyes like golden lamps. "Will you help me? Will you lift a hand to save yourselves from slavery and destruction? Or will you sit here quietly and await your doom?"

There was a pause. Finally Alys stirred. "I'm sorry," she said, "and I don't think you're evil anymore. But frankly I don't have the first idea what you're talking about."

The vixen sighed. "Of course you don't. I fully intend to explain." She hesitated a moment as if uncertain where to begin. Then she said, "I suppose you children have been taught to disbelieve in magic?"

"Well . . . ," said Alys.

"Of course you have. And rightly so. Because there is no magic—or precious little of it—in this world, *any-more*. But that doesn't mean there never was.

"The world where magic originated is called Findahl, the Wildworld. And it is, or was, connected to this world by countless Passages. The Quislais found the Passages first—well, they would! The Quislais are—oh, I suppose you people would call them fairies. Anyway, they wandered into the human world, and soon other Wildfolk followed—sorcerei and elementals and beasts you know only through legend.

"In those days the Wildfolk got along well enough with the people of Earth, which they called the Stillworld. But most were never really comfortable with your civilization.

And presently the humans turned against magic and began burning witches.

"The greatest sorcerei were too powerful to be caught, but many of the minor ones were killed, and witch-hunting proved to be the last straw for the Wildfolk. They decided to pull out of this world entirely.

"The Weerul Council, the supreme ruling body of Findahl, decreed that all the Wildfolk be evacuated at once to their own world, after which the Passages would be closed forever. Humans were to be sealed in the Stillworld and Wildfolk in the Wildworld, and there would never more be any congress between them. Plans were made immediately for enforcing this law, and of all those affected only one dared raise a voice in protest—Morgana." The vixen raised her head and eyed them grimly. "My mistress had always been something of a rebel, but this was more than that. You see, just before the Great Separation she fell in love with a young native American of the Yuma tribe, a dreamsinger. He was only a boy, but she loved him. And she wasn't about to give him up for anyone.

"The Weerul Council is powerful," continued the vixen, "but, oh, my mistress was clever! She went before them with a unique argument. You see, although Morgana's mother was a Quislai, her father was human, and she argued that by the Council's own decree she was obliged to spend half her time in the human world and half her time in the Wildworld.

"There was a tremendous debate about it, and Thia Pendriel, a magistrate of the Council, led the opposition. But in the end the Council ruled that a single Passage, the Great Coastal Passage by the Pacific, be left open and that Morgana be given control over it—on one condition. She had to keep it exclusively for her own use, and never, never let any humans through. The penalty for disobedience was death for both her and the human involved."

"Great Coastal Passage, huh?" said Charles curiously. "Where is it?"

"It's here, dolt!" said the vixen. "You're sitting on it! No, don't get up, you can't fall through accidentally. Morgana made sure of that. You see, she built this house directly over the Passage, and in the Wildworld, at the other end, she built another house, a counterpart. Then she tied up all the power of that great Passage and bent it to her will, and made it into a number of smaller passages connecting the two houses. And those passages are the mirrors."

"The mirrors," breathed Claudia.

"Yes. This is Fell Andred, the Mirror House, and you can walk through a mirror in this living room and emerge in the great hall of Morgana's castle in the Wildworld in one and a half seconds flat—if you have moonlight and the amulet.

"The amulet was Morgana's way of locking the Passage, of making it human-proof. She never told the secret of it to any of the other sorcerei. She settled down to live in this house with her new husband, and he willingly promised never to ask her where she went when she disappeared.

"But the young dreamsinger was human, and insatiably curious, and . . . well, you can guess the end of the story. He couldn't bear not knowing. He wheedled and cajoled and threatened and begged her until finally she made the amulet for him, and brought him into the Wildworld. And the long and the short of it is that he was caught there and Thia Pendriel had him put to death."

"Oh, *dear*," said Alys. She felt it was a foolish thing to say, but she couldn't help it.

The vixen ignored this. "Morgana herself was brought before the Council in chains. Of course, she didn't go quietly, and by the time she got there she had the deaths of quite a few minor sorcerei on her head. Thia Pendriel wanted Morgana cast into a Chaotic Zone, a place where the magic is so wild, so uncontrollable, that only a full Quislai could survive there and stay sane. There was a fight. The guardians of the High Council, the Feathered Serpents, soon ended that, but in the confusion Morgana managed to escape back to this world, where none of the sorcerei could follow her.

"The Council decided that the most merciful—and most practical—thing to do was commute Morgana's sentence to exile, with death as the penalty if she ever returned to the Wildworld. Morgana didn't care. She was half-mad with grief anyway, over the loss of her love. In anger and bitterness she flung down her Gold Staff and her grimoire, her great book of spells, and she locked her workshop and swore never to touch the mirrors or practice magic again. She kept that promise, too, until just a few days ago.

"Pay attention, now. I'm getting to the point." Before anyone could protest that they *were* paying attention, the vixen continued.

"All these many years since my mistress was exiled from the Wildworld she has been isolated from the

Wildfolk, all of them. Except Elwyn. Elwyn Silverhair, her half sister. Elwyn, daughter of a queen of fairies. Elwyn, the scatterbrained, light-minded, fickle-hearted, irresponsible nincompoop! If you can find one good thing to say about her I'll turn vegetarian! Amulets mean nothing to full Quislais. They are immortal and can cross any open Passage at will. The only thing that will hold a Quislai is a thornbranch tangled in the hair. And if amulets mean nothing, common decency means less. The mischief Elwyn has done! Luring young men into the Wildworld and dumping them back twenty years later, and setting loose dragons, and . . . Well. The less said about it the better. In any case, Morgana had no choice but to let her come and go as she pleased, and she often brought us news of the Wildworld, until about a century ago when she and Morgana had a terrible falling-out.

"We hadn't seen Elwyn since then, until last week, when she came tripping through a mirror as if she owned it, laughing like a loon, her long hair floating behind her. I don't know what she said to Morgana, but within ten minutes it developed into a magnificent fight. Elwyn threw a sky-bolt, and you can see what it did over there." Everyone turned to see that one wall of the living room was scarred and blackened in a circular area the size of a hula hoop.

"Morgana knows a trick or two of her own," added the vixen dryly, and for the first time her listeners took in the destruction around them: tables and chairs overturned and broken, rugs shredded, bric-a-brac scattered across the floor. "And Elwyn may be immune to pain or death or fear, but my mistress managed to chase her back to the Wildworld, all right. Much good it did! Next evening she returned and apologized in words so fair that I ought to have been suspicious right away. She and Morgana talked for hours behind a closed door, and the next thing I knew Morgana had gotten out her grimoire and was making up the amulet for herself and for me." The vixen stretched her neck, and they saw that she was wearing a golden collar with a little bag of green material tucked underneath.

"Then she told me that we would be going to the Wildworld that very night. Well, I was surprised, but I was ready at the time she appointed—an hour after sunset—only to find that she was already gone, and that wretched Elwyn with her.

"When she didn't return I realized something was wrong. The next day, at moonrise, I went through a mirror myself and, to my horror, I found the house full of the smell of strange sorcerei—and one scent that was all too familiar. Cadal Forge was there.

"I spied on him and listened to his counsels, and then I understood. *He* had persuaded Elwyn to lure Morgana into the Wildworld, and it is *he* who is holding Morgana prisoner. Why? Because his plans involve the mirrors, and in either world only Morgana can possibly close them against him.

"When I heard what his plans were I could scarcely credit my ears—but I should have realized, long ago, how twisted he had become. Morgana knew Cadal when he was a youth, the youngest wielder of a Red Staff in the Guild. Like her, he was dwelling in the human world. They shared a love of learning, and Cadal was actually apprenticed to a human alchemist—as close as you could get to a scientist in those days. But the Inquisition came and the alchemist betrayed Cadal to save his own life. The only thing your superstitious, blood-crazed ancestors hated more than science was sorcery, and they tortured Cadal before trying to burn him. Morgana rescued him from the stake itself and took him to the Wildworld to be healed, but the greatest wounds were not to his body.

"He turned against all humans. He took a terrible revenge on the poor alchemist, and when the Council announced the Plan for Separation he argued passionately that instead of withdrawing from the Stillworld the sorcerei should simply conquer it. The councillors wouldn't listen, of course, and eventually, after he intrigued against them once too often, they convicted him of treason. They cast him into a Chaotic Zone, but somehow he escaped, and I see now that he never gave up. He found other sorcerei of like mind and created a Society devoted to reentering and mastering the human world."

"But how could he get here?" said Charles. "I thought you said you needed the amulet to go through the mirrors."

"Very good. You do—*with one exception*. Do you know what the winter solstice is? The longest night of the year, which falls on December twenty-first—in just two weeks! Well, even Morgana could not tame the Passage completely, and on the night of the winter solstice, by light of a full moon that rises at midnight, it is open to all. From the moment the moon enters its quarter until the moment of dawn, anyone can cross over. Elwyn alone knew this, and she must have told Cadal Forge. Which means that in two weeks' time *he* will be coming through, with the rest of his Society. And he's got Morgana trapped in the Wildworld where she can't do a thing to stop him."

"But how can he keep her from coming back here?"

"He can kill her. . . . But since he hasn't done that yet I dare to hope that he will not. Still, I can think of a dozen ways. Unless you are a Quislai you need three things to cross through a mirror. The first is moonlight. Moonlight must fall on the mirror before you can go through. He could imprison her in a room with the windows boarded up, say, or bricked over. The second is the amulet. He could take that away from her, although hers wouldn't work for him. The third is the mirror itself. Obviously, if Morgana cannot reach a mirror she cannot pass through. He could weave a magic circle around her, or cast a binding spell, or simply tie her to a chair."

"Tie her to a *chair!*" said Janie. "If she's such a hot sorceress, why can't she free herself?"

"Why can't you hammer nails into a board with your elbow?" countered the vixen. "She went to the Wildworld in trust, without even her Gold Staff. A sorceress without her magic instruments is no more powerful than an ordinary woman. And that's why she needs our aid. I've gone through the mirrors every day since Morgana disappeared. I know she's in the castle somewhere, for I can smell it, but the rooms are so thick with enchantment it's hard to locate her precisely. The other sorcerei seem to have left for the time being. If you will help me, if you will go through the mirrors, too—"

"Us!" cried Claudia excitedly.

"Yes, you! Why do you think I've wasted all this time recounting the history of the Wildfolk? For my own amusement? I need help, and you four have able bodies and fair-to-middling minds. Or so I thought." The white teeth clicked together impatiently. "Well? Will you do it?

Will you help bring Morgana back to close the mirrors
once and for all?"

"I'll help," said Claudia instantly.

"Me, too," said Charles.

Alys still felt stunned and disoriented—and frightened.
She wished with all her heart that she had never come
with Claudia to the old house. She had a strange, almost
dreamlike desire to turn her back on the vixen, shut the
door behind her, and leave.

But whether she turned her back or not, the vixen
would still be there. And so would the house.

And the mirrors.

Slowly, she pushed a strand of long hair out of her eyes.
"All right," she said. "I'll do it. We'll do it."

The vixen, watching her with amber slits of eyes, inclined her head briefly. Alys couldn't tell if the gesture
was ironical or not.

Everyone turned to look at Janie. "Oh, I wouldn't miss
it for the world," said Janie with a smile. "But this Cadal
Forge—what makes you think he *can* take over the human world? We don't live in the Dark Ages anymore.
Technology—"

"Plague, famine, war—is technology going to save you
from those? He controls them all. Oh, don't you understand? The man holds a *Red Staff*. From the way he spoke
he means to set himself up as Lord of the Stillworld, with
the rest of his Society under him. Then they could use
you humans as they see fit. Listen to me. The alchemist
who betrayed him had a daughter, an innocent girl whom
Cadal once loved. When he killed the father he killed
her, too—in ways I will not mention. Once he has the

mastery of this world, what do you suppose he will do to *you?*"

After a short silence Alys spoke. "All right, but—I don't want to sound cowardly, but . . . why us? I mean, shouldn't you tell someone in authority?"

"And if I do? First of all, your 'authorities' will take me out of this house and put me in a cage for study. Here, as in the Wildworld, all true languages are one, but the minute they step outside that door they won't be able to understand a word I say. Second, they will seal this house and investigate it with all their top scientists and leading military personnel, and they will still be investigating like crazy when Cadal Forge comes through on the solstice. It's quite true that *you* stand no chance against him—but neither would any other human. It all depends upon Morgana."

"Oh," said Alys.

"Please," interposed Claudia. "Can I ask something? Are you from the Wildworld?"

When the vixen spoke again it was softly. "No. I am from this world. Centuries ago Morgana found a wounded fox kit in the woods, an ordinary animal left to die. She fed it and sheltered it and presently she gave it speech and the gift of long life." She paused, and for the first time the children felt how worried she was, and how sad. "We have been together since then."

With a return to her old brisk manner she added, "I must go through a mirror *now* and look for my mistress. Tell no one, especially no adults, of what has passed here, but be back tomorrow at moonrise, about three P.M. We must make the amulet."

"Wait," said Janie, as the vixen leapt sinuously off the

chair, "I haven't finished my questions. Why can't Morgana close the mirrors from the Wildworld side?"

"She needs the tools of her art, which are here. And if she closes herself in the Wildworld the Council will find her and kill her."

"Well, one more thing. What if you're wrong and Cadal Forge has killed her already?"

The vixen turned and clicked her teeth together gently. "Then," she said, "you are in a very great deal of trouble." With this she ran down the length of the living room and leapt toward the mirror which hung on the far wall. Everyone winced automatically, but although the mirror broke into a myriad of changing colors it offered no more resistance to her body than would a puff of air. The next instant she was gone.

chapter 4

THE POLICE

The next day Alys paced and frowned, Janie withdrew entirely, and Charles and Claudia pored eagerly over Charles's old magic books, looking for "internal evidence of the Wildworld." No one went anywhere until three o'clock, when, with one accord, all four children made a dash for their bikes and raced down the road to the old house on the hill.

And the vixen wasn't there.

They waited for her. Alys, who had felt some nameless dread all day, was unable to stand still. She took a tour of the enormous living room, whose ceiling was three stories high, with open galleries circling the walls at the second and third levels. When she returned she found Charles and Claudia making forts of scattered cushions and Janie examining the mirror the vixen had gone through. To

Alys's horror she was examining it by scratching it with their mother's diamond engagement ring.

They waited until the shadows outside grew long. At last, feeling that if she did not *do* something she would lose her mind, Alys suggested that they search the house.

It reminded her of some mad Easter-egg hunt as they dashed around, looking behind draperies and into chests and wardrobes. The house was so large that at the end of the search they could not be sure they had even seen every room, but one thing was certain. They had not found the vixen.

"What do we do now?" Claudia looked at Alys with total confidence as they returned to the living room.

Alys stirred uneasily and shot a sideways glance at Janie. Janie, she knew, had come to the same conclusion as she had. But Janie was not to be relied upon for help.

"I think," she said slowly, "that the only thing we can do . . . is go to the police."

Charles and Claudia stared at her, aghast.

"But the vixen said, about grown-ups, not to tell them!"

"I know, Claudia, and if the vixen were here I'd do it her way. But the point is she isn't here. And this thing is serious. It's *beyond* us. I can't be responsible for it."

"But when the vixen comes back—"

"The vixen isn't *coming* back," interrupted Janie harshly. "Don't you realize that? The only thing that would have kept her from coming today is if she was captured—or killed. Probably killed. Face it, Claudia, the vixen is probably *dead*." Claudia's face looked stricken.

"*Janie, you shut up*," said Alys furiously. "You just love

to see people miserable, don't you?" she added between her teeth as she took Claudia in her arms.

Janie flushed, then her purple eyes went cold as ice. She settled back in her chair without another word.

Charles ignored all this. "Alys, if we tell the police what's happened they'll think we're raving lunatics."

"I thought of that." Releasing Claudia gently, Alys began pacing up and down the room. "But if I talk very slowly and sensibly, and tell the story from the beginning—"

"—they'll give you a nice shot of sedative and put you in a rubber room. Come on! Did *you* believe Claudia when she first told us about a magic vixen? And she's our sister!"

Alys looked helplessly at Janie, but Janie's pointed face was like carven stone. "If we had some evidence—"

"But we *don't* have any evidence. That's the problem. And we're just kids, and they're never going to listen."

Alys tugged at her hair distractedly. Her pacing brought her up against an old-fashioned rolltop desk, and she stared down at it, unseeing. Or—perhaps not quite unseeing, for a moment later she found that one particular item on the desk stood out distinctly.

A wild inspiration formed in her brain. Slowly, she turned back to her brother.

"Charles . . . what if we could make them believe us? What if we *did* have some evidence?"

"What if pigs flew?"

"What if "—Alys picked up an ancient quill pen from the desk and twirled it at him—"we had a letter from Morgana?"

* * *

The last thing Alys said before leaving for the police station was, "I'd appreciate it if you washed your face, Claudia. And, Charles, I don't think that unprintable slogan on your T-shirt is going to help the cause."

Once decided, it had all been so simple. Alys was not artistic like Charles, but she had one talent which made her the envy of all her friends, especially those friends who had frequent unexcused absences at school. She could forge anybody's handwriting.

It was a gift ideally suited to practical jokes. Alys's teachers found, to their astonishment, that they had written long complimentary comments on mediocre schoolwork. Friends got love notes from boys who didn't remember writing them. So far Alys, being Alys, had never used her ability for anything more serious than a prank. But now . . .

Of course, they didn't have a specimen of Morgana's writing. But Alys had taken a calligraphy class last summer in which she had learned to use an old-fashioned pen and inkwell, and when the letter was finished it certainly didn't look like anything written by a teenager.

The contents were straightforward. This letter was written by Morgana Shee, to be unsealed (they had found wax and a seal in the desk) in the case of her death or disappearance. Inside, it told the story as the vixen had told it to them, ending with a plea for help. When Alys finished the letter she placed it partially hidden under the rolltop of the desk, because she thought it would be better if the police found it themselves when they searched the house. It happened that way in movies.

Once Alys was gone Charles took off his shirt and put

32

it on inside out, so the slogan didn't show, and then he forcibly washed Claudia in the kitchen sink.

"But you still don't look respectable," he said afterward. Claudia's brown hair was even more tousled than usual, and her eyes and nose were red and swollen. With only a little trouble he persuaded her to hide in the kitchen when the police came.

It seemed a long time before they heard a car on the driveway. Charles got to the door just as it opened, then gave way before the tide of two policemen. Alys was pale, with only a spot of color in each cheek, but she nodded at him triumphantly.

"You see," she said to the policemen, "this is just the way we found the house. It's pretty bad, isn't it?"

"Mmm-hmm," said the taller policeman, taking in the destruction of the room. He looked at Charles. "So what do you know about this?"

"I guess Alys already told you," said Charles uncomfortably. The shorter policeman was looking around, but he wasn't looking very carefully, and he was heading for the kitchen. Charles craned his neck to follow him.

"Don't worry about him. Just tell me in your own words what happened," said the tall policeman, and Charles managed somehow to stumble through the story about the vixen. "I know it sounds crazy, impossible, but I swear it's the truth," he finished.

"Mmm-hmm," said the policeman again.

Alys was standing by the desk, where just a corner of the letter could be seen. "Don't you think," she said, "that you should—well, look around the house or something?"

Just at that moment the short policeman emerged from

the kitchen, holding Claudia by the arm. "Here's another one."

The two officers bent over Claudia, murmuring, and Alys shot an anxious glance at Charles. Then, looking very hard the other way, she caught the corner of the letter with her fingertips and pulled it further into sight. So far, she had to admit, things weren't going very well. The police had *listened* to her, yes, and they had come with her, but as to whether they *believed* her or not . . . Well, the letter would help.

"What was that?" she said, snatching her fingers away, as one of the policemen spoke to her. "Oh, yes, I know it's late for Claudia to be out." She was blushing furiously. Worse, they weren't searching the house; they weren't going to discover the letter. Hadn't they ever seen any murder mysteries on TV? Wretchedly, behind her back, she tugged at the letter again, and felt it flutter to the floor. She made a grab for it, bent, and straightened to find both policemen looking directly at her.

"L-look what I found," she choked out.

The tall policeman tore the envelope open silently and read. Then he handed the letter to the other one.

Alys's face cooled in the silence that followed, and the knot in her stomach relaxed a little. The letter was good, awfully good; she knew that. She'd had enough practice amazing her friends at parties, seen enough reactions of grown-ups, to know just how good she was.

The second policeman finished reading, and the two of them exchanged a glance over Alys's head.

"I'd say," said the tall one, "that this looks pretty serious."

"*Yes*," said Alys, with forced calm, her heart lifting.

"I wonder," he continued, taking a small notebook out of his pocket, "if before we take this back to the station for evidence, you would each write a sample sentence for me?"

There was a moment of absolute silence.

"What—what do you mean? What sentence?" said Alys at last.

"Oh, how about this one here, 'to be opened in case of my death or disappearance,' " said the policeman quietly.

Everything blurred around Alys. The meaning of this was unmistakable—and unbelievable. No one else had ever been so skeptical, not even teachers confronted with their own handwriting. No one had immediately asked to compare it to hers.

But—wait. What good would comparison do? The calligraphic characters in the letter were nothing at all like her normal writing. As first Janie, then Charles, then Claudia took the pen the policeman was pressing on them, Alys tried desperately to quiet her heart and *think*.

Could they tell or couldn't they? She had to know.

"Can I—can I just ask why you want us to do that?" she asked shakily. "I mean, if you think one of us wrote that letter—well, we'd *disguise* our handwriting, wouldn't we?"

"No one," said the policeman, "can disguise handwriting enough to fool an expert."

And that, of course, was that. Alys felt somehow she should have known all along. Meanwhile, everyone was looking at her; Claudia had produced some illegible chicken scratches on the pad, and the tall policeman was holding out the pen.

She could not hope for help, and no help came. Janie's

expressionless face, Charles's miserable one, seemed unnaturally bright and faraway. For a moment the best thing she could think of doing was to run.

Her hand fell away from the pen.

"I wrote the letter," she whispered.

"I see," said the policeman in a hateful, smug voice.

"But it's true—all the rest of it—everything we said!" The words came in a flood, like the tears that suddenly streamed down her cheeks uncontrollably. "It is, it *is*. We just didn't know how to make you believe us. We—"

"You wanted to be believed, so you forged this letter and lied. Is that it?"

"Yes—no—" Tears and confusion overcame her.

"Anyway, look at this place." Charles had gotten his breath back and was now pointing to the burn the skybolt had made on the wall. "It's trashed. Isn't that evidence enough?"

"How'd it happen, son? Fireworks?"

For the first time since the police had entered, Janie spoke. "Have you ever seen a firework that could do *that?*"

"Mexican kind. Illegal."

As Charles spun away in disgust, the tall policeman took Alys by the arm. In a very few minutes they were all outside.

"Now," said the policeman, and as they stood on the paved courtyard in the moonlight he proceeded to tell them, in words they would never forget, just how little the Law was amused by this kind of practical joke.

"In fact," he said, softly, "I think this goes further than a joke. I think whoever wrecked that house was attempting arson. There's been a lot of vandalism around here recently, most of it down by the schools, but some of it up as far as these hills. If I had a single scrap of evidence to connect you with what I saw in there you'd be on your way to Juvenile Hall right now. As it is, I'm giving you just one minute to get on your bikes and disappear. And I don't ever—and I repeat *ever*—want to see you within five hundred yards of this place again. Get it? Now, move!"

Charles pulled Alys toward their bikes. There was nothing else to do.

chapter 5

THE SPELL

Don't cry, Al," said Charles, when they had turned off onto the first side street from Morgana's. Alys was standing exactly where she'd come to rest, straddling her bicycle, her face buried in her hands. Charles looked away in embarrassment and addressed a bougainvillea bush across the street. "You did your best," he told the bush. "You *tried*."

Alys's shoulders heaved and she said nothing. Claudia leaned over to put a small, sweaty hand on her arm.

"Anyway," said Charles, "it was a good idea."

"It was a terrible idea," said Janie. "Of course an expert graphologist would be able to tell she wrote it."

These words accomplished what Charles's solace and Claudia's sympathy had not. Alys raised her head.

"You knew that?" She looked at Janie through swollen

eyelids and Janie exhaled sharply and looked away, lips compressed. "And you just stood by and let me go ahead?"

Janie turned back and met her gaze defiantly.

"Next time, don't tell me to shut up," she said.

"You *crud*—" began Charles, but Alys broke in.

"Right, Miss Genius," she said. "Well, while you were standing aside and having yourself a good laugh, did it ever occur to you that our only chance of help was disappearing forever? And that the solstice is only twelve days away? And that now it's up to *us?*" Alys shook her head hard, once, then turned to Charles and Claudia.

"Okay," she said. "You were right and I was wrong. Let's go."

"What? *Where?*" said Janie.

"Back to the old house, of course."

"But what can we *do?*"

"I don't know," said Alys. "But someone has got to do something."

"And what about the police? They said we weren't supposed to go within five hundred yards of that house."

Alys smiled faintly for the first time in a long while.

"Actually," she said, "they said they didn't want to *find* us within five hundred yards of the house. And they won't. We'll see to that."

"But—"

"No one," said Alys, "is forcing you to come."

But Janie did come, walking her bike slowly behind the others with an odd, set look on her face.

"The vixen said the spell for making the amulet is written down somewhere," said Alys, when they were inside the house again.

"In a grimoire," said Charles. "What *is* a grimoire, anyway?"

Claudia leaned a little closer to Alys. "Is it a big book?" she asked huskily. "A great big book on a stand with funny handwriting in it and a black cover?"

"Yes, very likely," said Alys, turning back to Charles. "It's a book of spells, and what we have to do—" She stopped. "What do you mean, 'Is it a great big book on a stand with a black cover?'" she asked Claudia.

"I found one like that in a little room beside the kitchen," said Claudia simply. "When Charles sent me there to wait. I didn't know what it was."

Janie was looking at Alys with unconcealed horror. "And so we're just going to whip up a spell on our own, is that it? As if it were a recipe for banana bread?"

"We don't have any choice. You saw to that."

The grimoire turned out to be the largest book they had ever seen, with pages made of parchment illuminated with tracery, and it was open to a page thickly covered with elegant, intricate writing. The problem was they couldn't read the writing.

"Latin?" said Alys doubtfully, once they had carried the book between them to the kitchen table where there was light. The script was fine and beautiful but so crowded together it was impossible to distinguish individual words.

"Why Latin?" said Charles. "If you want old, there's plenty of languages older than that. It could be, uh, Greek, or Babylonian, or Egyptian hieroglyphs."

Claudia was dismayed. "You mean we can't do the spell?"

They all stared at the book unhappily.

"I hate to say this," said Charles. "But those letters don't even look like our alphabet to me."

"I know," said Alys. "Well, maybe it *is* Greek. Or Russian. Russian's in another alphabet, Cyrillic or something, isn't it, Janie? Janie?"

Janie had been gazing at the writing as intently as the others, but now she gave a little start and blinked. "It's not Cyrillic," she murmured and abruptly got up and went to stand by the window.

Alys gave her an exasperated glare and returned to the page. The words didn't look Greek to her; they looked even stranger, more alien and unreadable. Yet they also had an air of mocking familiarity, and she felt she would be able to read them if she only looked at them the right way.

"What we need," said Charles lugubriously, "is a what-do-you-call-it, a person who studies languages."

"Um." Alys's eyes hurt from staring. When she absently raised her head to blink at him something caught her attention. "What on earth did you do to your T-shirt?"

"Turned it inside out. You said . . ."

"I know. But I can still read the slogan."

Charles tucked his chin under to look. "You can?"

"Yes." The black letters were plainly visible through the thin white cotton. "It's just backward—" Alys broke off, her eyes widening. "Backward!" she exclaimed, snapping her head down to look at the page. "Backward!"

"What?"

"It's English! The spell! It's English *backward!*"

"Not backward," said Janie quietly, turning. "It's reversed. A mirror image."

Alys stared at her in disbelief. When she spoke, her voice matched Janie's quiet tone. "So you knew that, Janie. Why didn't you tell us?"

"Because," said Janie, holding her gaze, "I have some very serious reservations about this whole business."

Charles and Claudia were bent over the grimoire, Charles trying to spell out the turned-around letters which ran from right to left. " 'For . . . the . . . uh . . . T-r-a-v . . . For the Travels . . .' "

" 'For the Traversal of the Mirrors,' " said Janie, still engaged in a stare-down with Alys.

"Hey, that's right! This is the one!" Charles began spelling out the next line, but Alys interrupted him. "We need a mirror, so we can look at the reflection of this writing in it. Claude, try to find a small one; I'll get a pencil."

Halfway through copying the spell Alys stopped and stared, checking her writing several times against the mirror reflection. The grim look did not leave her face even when she finished the copying and put down the pencil.

"What's the matter?" said Charles.

"You'll see. Read it."

Charles took the sheet of paper covered with Alys's own neat round handwriting, and read:

"For the Traversal of the Mirrors. Be drest in pure virgyn garments fromme head to heel, and girt with a red girdel of pleached corde, and shodde in blue. Take each ingredient belowe, and put it in a mortar, and grynde it all fine till it be enough. Then bring the pouder forthe and put it in a crucible of golde. Add thereto the blood and spittle of ye who wolde

traverse the mirrors. Stir widdershins and wake with the first reflexion of moonrise. When cool, parte and sew into bagges of green silke. Wear at the neck.''

"That's it," said Charles. "Then there's just a list of ingredients. So what's wrong?"

"Read the ingredients," said Alys.

"Oh. Okay. It says we need, uh, dwaleberry and red wulfenite, quicksilver and peacock coal, hornblende and wild elephant's ear, stinking smut and bladderwort, fly-club and phoenix feather and sunfish scales and falcon's tooth and . . ." He broke off, looking unhappy. "It says —a shard of human bone."

"What's a shard?" asked Claudia.

"A little piece," said Janie. "Like a splinter."

"Jeez, Alys, are you sure you transcribed this right? I mean *human* bone? How're we going to get hold of that?"

"Oh, well," said Janie, suddenly cheerful. "There's always the obvious solution."

"Which is?"

"Well, we all have bones, don't we? It would only take a little one. Like this." Janie grabbed Claudia's pinky finger. "This is a nice little bone, just the size of a shard," she said ghoulishly.

"Janie!"

"You wouldn't mind, would you, Claude? Maybe Mom would give you some anesthetic. It would be over in a minute."

Janie leaned forward, smiling madly at the cowering Claudia.

"Janie, shut up!"

"I told you not to—"

"About the other ingredients," said Charles, placing himself and the list between his sisters. "Some of these sound just as bad."

"I know. The first thing is to find out what they are. Remember, these are old-fashioned names. We'll divide the list up and each research a part. Once we know what we're looking for we can figure out how to get it."

So the list was divided, and because Claudia wanted to help out, Alys gave her the top ingredient, dwaleberry, and had Janie copy the next four for herself. Janie did this without expression, but as she rose to leave she wiggled her fingers under Claudia's nose.

"Don't forget, Claude," she said. "I mean, it's not as if you were ever going to play piano or anything."

"Do I have to copy this?" Charles said as she left the kitchen. "Or can I just tear it in half?"

"Copy," said Alys positively, standing up. "Just a sec." She caught up with Janie at the back door.

"Now, Alys," said Janie, looking at her speculatively, "I hope you're going to keep your sense of humor. I hope you're not going to say—"

"I've got only one thing to say," said Alys. "And it's this. If you don't lay off Claudia at once and forevermore I am going to knock your head off."

Janie's mouth fell open.

"I may not be a genius," Alys continued, "but if there's one thing I know about it's teamwork. And you have to decide right now whether or not you're on our team. If you don't want to help us, if you're scared, that's fine. But if you plan on working with us, you're going to act like one of us. You're going to *try* to help, and if you have any bright ideas you're going to tell us right away. Because if you don't I am going to pull your brains out through your nostrils. Understand?"

Janie's mouth opened and shut like a fish's.

"Good. Off you go, then." Alys turned on her heel and marched back into the house.

The next afternoon they gathered in the kitchen once more. They'd done well with their research: Even Claudia had found out that dwaleberry was another name for deadly nightshade, or *atropa belladona*. They now knew that quicksilver was mercury, that red wulfenite, peacock coal, and hornblende were all minerals, that wild elephant's ear, bladderwort, and stinking smut were plants, and that sunfish scales, flyclub, and phoenix feather were parts of animals. But, as Charles said, knowing and getting were two different things.

"I called that big nursery on Tustin where Dad bought his sago palm," he told Alys, "and they don't even have any of these plants. The guy just laughed when I asked about bladderwort and elephant's ear, and when I got to stinking smut he hung up. And about the other ingredients—how many do you really think we can get hold of, three or four? Much less the human bone."

At the mention of the bone everyone looked quickly at Janie, but she seemed to be studying her own list intently. "I'll tell you something else," she said without looking up. "I got a book on witchcraft, and according to it witches gather their own herbs. By moonlight. Naked."

"Naked!" said Charles.

"Skyclad, they call it. And there may be special incantations to be said. . . . Alys, you're not paying attention."

"No," said Alys. "I'm sorry. But Charles is right. We'll never be able to dig up half these things, naked or not."

Janie looked at her quickly. "You mean you're giving up?"

chapter 6

THE HIDDEN ROOM

No! Of course I'm not giving up," said Alys. "But I've been thinking all day and we're going about this wrong. The vixen expected us to mix up the amulet in one afternoon, like Morgana did. If the ingredients were that hard to find she'd be expecting the impossible."

"Maybe they're growing in the garden," said Charles.

"Not wulfenite and peacock coal and hornblende, they're not. But *think*. Where does a sorceress get the ingredients for her spells? She can't cross the Atlantic every time she needs European dwaleberry. She doesn't keep a nest of falcon chicks or a bowl of sunfish—"

"A laboratory!" A sudden light came into Janie's purple eyes. "She'd have a laboratory of her own. Or at least a storeroom for her stuff. I bet it's right here in the house. Hidden, maybe, behind a false wall—"

"The cellar!" cried Charles.

"Damp," said Janie. "Drafty."

"Witches like drafts."

"The towers!" squealed Claudia, knocking over a chair as she bolted out of the kitchen. Charles bolted the other way.

"Wait a minute, let's get organized," said Alys, but they were gone. She looked at Janie, who was wearing quite a different expression than she had been these last few days.

"Faust did it in a library," Janie said thoughtfully.

"There's a library on the second floor," said Alys. "I'll go up there. You do this floor. Try not to get lost."

Alys's warning to Janie was quite serious. There were so many dozens of rooms in the old house, and so many unexpected twists and turnings, that it was easy to lose the way.

The house was built like a hollow square enclosing a courtyard. The south and west sides of the quadrangle had been closed off. When their doors were forced they revealed whole wings of little rooms which looked as if they had not been entered for centuries. All were empty.

On the north side, the ancient, smoke-stained kitchen opened into the three-story living room, which was easily the largest room in the house. The east side was where Alys and Janie were going now. Leaving the first-story rooms to Janie, Alys went up the spiral staircase in the northeast tower to the second story.

She emerged in a high arched hallway which looked down on the courtyard on the right and had a range of doors on the left. The first door opened on Morgana's bedchamber, which was dominated by a magnificent canopy bed hung with velvet draperies. In a recess, standing opposite one another, were two full-length mirrors. When Alys stood between these they reflected her, front and back, to infinity, so that the room seemed full of people.

The second room down the gallery had been converted to a study, the third was a sitting room, the fourth was the library, and the fifth held a great spinning wheel. Each had its own mirror; some were beautiful, like the polished bronze sitting-room mirror, some ugly and strange, like the study mirror which was so tarnished Alys could scarcely see herself in it. Nowhere could she find any sign of a secret panel or hidden doorway.

The sixth room was different from the others. It was entirely bare: no tapestries, no wardrobe, not even a candle in the alcove. Only a very small bed pushed away in one corner.

It looks like a child's bed, thought Alys, and she wondered if Morgana had ever had a child, and if so why this room, this nursery, was now so empty. It looked almost as if someone had stripped it clean in anger, throwing away anything that might spark a memory.

Her thoughts were interrupted by a shout from the tower. "Alys, come quick! Charles says he's found it."

She ran into Janie, who was doing the shouting, in the hallway, and they both hurried down the stairs and back to the kitchen. Here a long, narrow staircase led to the cellar.

Claudia was already down there, and she and Charles had their ears pressed to one wall. Close by them, glowing in the red sunlight that came through a small window set just above ground level, was a rusty mirror.

"Listen!" Excitedly, Charles beckoned them closer. With his other hand he thumped several times slowly on the wall, while Claudia added a furious counterpart of quick rappings.

"Now listen," he said, and reaching an arm's length away he knocked again. This time the sound was different.

"And look!" he added. "You can see the outline, sort of, if you stand right. This crack is the side, and that one up there is the top. It's a door."

"And this is the keyhole," said Claudia. She had four small fingers stuck in a knothole.

"Wait a minute," said Janie. Nudging Claudia out of the way, she slipped sensitive fingers almost as small as her sister's into the hole. "There's metal in here. . . . It's some kind of a lock. If I can just push it right . . ."

With a soft *click* an entire section of the wall swung inward.

The small room thus revealed was illuminated by slit-shaped windows at ground level, and it had a mirror. Every inch of wall that wasn't window or mirror was shelves. And every shelf, from floor to ceiling, was stacked with rows and rows and rows of bottles and jars and vials and phials and retorts.

"Wow," said Claudia.

"I'll bet half of those are poisonous," said Janie.

"I told you witches like drafts," said Charles.

Alys's sense of triumph was tempered with awe at the sheer quantity of bottles which shone in the last rays of the setting sun. "I'm afraid it will take us hours—" she began, but Claudia interrupted.

"Footprints!" she said, pointing.

It was true; the thick carpet of dust on the floor clearly showed a single set of footprints leading to the shelves and back.

"Morgana!" said Claudia, hugging herself with delight.

"Sure has little feet," said Charles critically.

Janie, who had already stepped into the room to examine one wall of shelves, suddenly made a strangled sound.

"Alys. *Alys*. *Alys*."

"Black widow!" cried Charles instantly, leaping to her side. "Where'd it bite you?"

Janie pushed him away and stumbled toward Alys. Her eyes were wild.

"Alys!"

"Take a deep breath and try again. Count to three."

Janie clutched her by the shirt and towed her to the wall. "Alys, look. Look, Alys." she said in a terribly controlled voice. "They're not labeled. No labels. Do you know what that *means*?"

"Sweet heavens," whispered Alys, sitting down on the floor.

Everyone looked at the rows of shelves that towered above them, each shelf bristling with unlabeled containers.

"There must be a million of 'em," said Charles.

"Probably only a few thousand. But it might as well be a million," said Alys.

Claudia's lower lip trembled. Alys gathered her into one arm, shaking her head. They had come so close. Numbly, she took a bottle from the nearest shelf, one just off the floor. Inside the dusty glass she could see the wink of greenish powder. It could have been peacock coal for all she knew, or ground elephant's ear, or essence of deadly nightshade.

Charles, across the room, was whistling aimlessly. He took a bottle, shook it, peered at it, then replaced it. He looked up at the next shelf, and the one after that. He slapped his thighs a few times with open hands, flexing his knees. He picked up another bottle.

"Don't breathe it," said Alys automatically, as he tried to take the stopper out. "It might be poisonous."

"I can't even open it," said Charles, struggling. "The cork's in tight."

Alys twisted the glass stopper of her own bottle. "Mine, too."

"Vacuum packed," said Charles with a weak grin, and he bent to rap the bottle on the stone floor. "That's got it," he said as the stopper came free.

"Good idea," said Alys, rapping her own bottle.

"Stop!" shrieked Janie. "Don't anybody move! Charles, don't put that bottle back!"

"Janie," began Alys mildly.

"Hold on to those bottles! Don't forget which ones they are! Oh, don't you see?" she cried as the others stared at her. "They're sealed. They're vacuum-packed. None of them has been opened in five hundred years. Except—"

"Holy cripes!" said Charles, astonished.

"Janie," said Alys, "you *are* a genius. Claudia, do you understand? All we have to do now is try all the bottles, and the ones that open are the ones holding what Morgana put into the amulet. We did it. We actually did it!" She hugged Claudia hard, and Charles shouted, and even Janie smiled.

"But now we've got to work," said Alys briskly. "We need some chairs to reach the higher shelves—"

"I'll get them," said Charles.

"—and some candles, too. It's so dark that—omigosh! It's dark! *Dinner!*"

There was a mad rush for the stairs.

They ate dinner in a daze. Their parents were more than a little bemused by their sudden urgent desire for one another's company. It had been years, commented Dr. Hodges-Bradley, since all four of her children had spent an afternoon together.

"It's—it's a surprise," said Alys. "You know, Dad's birthday is coming. We're working on it again tonight."

Mr. Hodges-Bradley looked pleased.

"Why, darlings, how nice of you," said their mother. "But even so, I don't want Claudia out late."

"Late, late, what's late?" gabbled Alys, seeing Claudia's mouth open to its widest in preparation for a yell.

"You know her bedtime is eight o'clock."

"Eight? Eight? How about eight-thirty?" Claudia was now as purple as a beet. Charles was doing something to her under the table to keep her quiet, but he wouldn't be able to restrain her long.

"It's only this one night," continued Alys feverishly. "I'll take care of her, Mom. Please, just for one night."

Dr. Hodges-Bradley blinked. "Well . . . if it's that important to you. But, remember, tomorrow's a school day."

So Claudia went with them back to Morgana's secret storeroom. They brought from home the emergency candles from the kitchen cupboard and Claudia's Santa

Claus candle that had never been lit and Alys's camping flashlight. Alys and Charles stood on chairs and tested the upper shelves; Janie and Claudia took the lower ones.

Alys made the first find, a bottle of bright golden feathers, whose stopper yielded easily to her hand. Triumphantly, she passed it down to Janie. Then Claudia found a bottle full of red crystals. Then Alys found another bottle, then Charles. Soon they were flying through the shelves.

"Uh-oh," said Charles once, and Alys looked at him.

"An empty," he said.

Janie moved to his side and Alys went on testing bottles. She had a terrible feeling about that empty. Maybe it had contained something easy like quicksilver or flyclub —but she didn't think so.

Janie told them when they had gathered thirteen bottles, but they went ahead and tested the rest anyway. Janie said it would help prove their hypothesis. Alys was hoping they would find another bottle to make up for that empty.

All the other stoppers were in tight. At last, with a crick in her neck, Alys stepped down from her chair.

"Well?" she said to Janie.

"We have exactly thirteen bottles. Problem: Twelve are full, one is empty. Question: Which one?"

At Janie's suggestion, they took the bottles to the kitchen and let her sort them. "Because," she said, "if we can figure out what we *do* have, we can tell what we *don't* have." Janie opened every jar, and when she was satisfied she'd identified one she made a check on the master list of ingredients. At last she'd examined all the bottles.

"It's just what you'd expect," she said wearily, sitting

back. "I can't be sure of telling those plants from one another, but I do know we've got all four. The feathers and the mercury are easy. The minerals are easy. These little brown things I think are flyclub, and the bright things are sunfish scales. Which leaves . . ."

"The human bone. Naturally."

"So we're back where we started," said Charles.

"Not exactly," said Janie. "We have twelve out of thirteen ingredients."

"Yes, and how are we going to get the thirteenth?"

"There are ways," said Janie, but she didn't say it very loudly.

After that, conversation languished.

Early the next morning Charles knocked at the door of his mother's darkroom.

"Come on in." His mother was bent over the sink, her fair hair coppery in the red light. "What is it?"

"Mmmm," said Charles, studying the ceiling with elaborate casualness. Then: "Say, Mom, do you get many broken bones at the office?"

"A few," said his mother, amused.

"Well," said Charles, "I mean, like, do you ever get people whose bones are sticking out of their skin? And maybe little splinters breaking off?"

"Cases like that go straight to the emergency room of a hospital. Why on *earth* do you want to know?"

"Oh, I just wondered," Charles said vaguely. He wandered out again. He knew perfectly well what Alys would say, but he mentioned his idea to her anyway over breakfast.

Alys said it. "We are not going to lurk around any hospitals looking for injured people. You're as bad as Janie."

Charles shrugged.

chapter 7

A SHARD OF
HUMAN BONE

On the way to school, Alys said, "We need money."

"Don't tell me. We're going to hire some grave robbers," said Charles.

"No, I'm serious. Even if we don't have the you-know-what there's plenty of other equipment we need to actually mix up the amulet. The crucible of gold, for instance—"

"—is in Morgana's sink," said Charles. "So are the mortar and pestle."

"All right, but we still need the 'red girdel of pleached corde,' and the blue shoes—that's what 'shodde in blue' means, you know. According to Janie's book, the 'girdel' isn't an eighteen-hour girdle, it's just a belt. And 'pleached' means braided. So it looks like we have to buy red cord to braid. Plus, the book says that pure virgin garments are clothes that have never been worn, and although I suppose we can dig up one set of new clothes between us, the shoes we have to buy."

"I've got blue tennis shoes," offered Claudia.

Alys shook her head. "They've been worn. And we also have to buy green silk to make the bags, and silk isn't cheap."

Charles sighed heavily. "All right, all right," he said. "Dr. Foster did ask me if I could watch Kevin and Amy this afternoon so they don't have to stay in day care. I wasn't going to do it because that dog of theirs makes a break for freedom every time I open the door, and usually Kevin bites me. But if we really need money I will."

So after school Charles rode his bike to the Fosters', which was on Center Street, almost at the foot of Morgana's hill. Professor Foster, who taught at the University of California at Irvine, promised to be back by dinnertime. He also warned Charles—as if Charles needed any warning—not to let Zochimilcho, the Great Dane, into the house while the cat was inside.

Kevin and Amy gave no more than the usual trouble, and by six o'clock Charles began to look for the professor's return. He'd promised to meet Alys and the others at the old house. By six-thirty it was clear that the faculty meeting was running late, so Charles gave the kids a choice of bologna sandwiches or Wheaties for dinner and settled down with the cat to watch TV. At seven Janie showed up, looking cross.

"It's not my fault," said Charles. "He said he'd be home

by now. A lot of thanks I get for spending the whole afternoon with two screaming kids and a rabid dog."

Janie shot a critical look at Zochimilcho, who was testing the stress factor of the sliding glass door by hurling himself headlong against it. "Hyperactive," she commented, and went to study a collection of Aztec artifacts in a glass case on the wall.

"He's an anthropologist, isn't he?" she asked.

"The *dog?*"

"Never mind. Where's the bathroom?"

"First door down the hall after the professor's study."

Janie was gone for several minutes. Charles flicked the TV from channel to channel.

As Janie returned he heard a car outside. "See?" he said, turning off the TV and going to the window. "He's back already. If you—what's wrong?"

"Charles—are you sure he's back?"

"Yeah, and he's got some other people with him. Want to help me clean up Kevin and Amy?" He stepped into the playroom, but Janie stood quite still in the middle of the living room floor. Nor did she move when Charles herded Kevin and Amy out, and Dr. Foster and his guests came in.

"Sorry to be late," said the professor to Charles, and, "Hello, you're Charles's sister, aren't you?" to Janie.

"Yes," said Janie. She was making queer agitated movements with her head and shoulders. Charles had the feeling she was trying to convey some message to him, but he had no idea what.

"What do I owe you?" resumed the professor to Charles. "Let's see, I've got some small bills in the study." He moved off, with Kevin and Amy trailing behind. The guests stood in the entry hall. Janie, to Charles's surprise, walked over to the sliding glass door.

"Go with him," she hissed at Charles.

"What?"

"Keep him *occupied.*"

Bewildered but obedient, Charles headed for the hall. An instant later he froze, horrified, as he heard the unmistakable sound of a glass door opening. There was a terrific baying as Zochimilcho exploded into the house and promptly crashed into the dining room table.

"What the—" From behind Charles, Dr. Foster came running. Charles, still paralyzed in the hallway, blocked him long enough for Zochimilcho to gain the living room. There was a wavering feline howl and then another crash.

"Bad dog! Zochi! No! I said, nooooo!" Dr. Foster pushed past Charles into the living room. He could hardly be heard above all the other sounds. Charles turned furiously on Janie for an explanation, but she was elbowing her way past Dr. Foster's guests.

"I have to go to the bathroom," she said, although no one seemed to be listening.

"Bad dog! Be quiet, Zochi! Who let him *in?*" Dr. Foster was roaring from the living room. Charles hastily went to help him drag Zochimilcho into the yard.

"My sister let him in, sir," he said then, wretchedly. "She—well, I guess she didn't know any better."

"Of all the stupid—next time you *tell* her! Oh, well, no real harm done, I guess," he added, seeing Charles's face. "That was my dog, Zochimilcho!" he shouted to his guests. There seemed to be a certain note of pride in his voice.

The mention of Janie had made Charles look around apprehensively. Where was she? Not in the bathroom, he was sure of that.

"Good-bye, Charles," chorused Amy and Kevin sweetly as Dr. Foster walked him to the door. To Charles's relief Janie reappeared at that moment.

"Good-bye, good-bye, professor," she said, sidestepping Kevin. "Good-bye," she said again, giving Charles a violent shove which landed them both outside before Dr. Foster could say a word. The last Charles saw of the professor he was standing in the doorway, shaking his head.

"What was that about?" he hissed at Janie, jerking his arm away. Her bike stood by his on the driveway.

"Shut up; we've got to get out of here," she snarled back. "*Hurry*, Charles." She was on her bike in a flash, launching herself toward the street, rising off the seat to put more muscle into her pedaling. It took Charles a minute or so to catch up with her—with Janie!—she was pumping at such a furious pace toward the hill.

"Are you crazy?" he shouted as he drew alongside her.

Janie glared at him, nearly ran into a parked car, and refused to answer. She was ahead of him all the way to Morgana's, and only when they were standing under the beams of the ancient, smoke-stained kitchen, with Alys and Claudia staring at them, did she speak.

"I've done it," she said. "And he'll probably find out and send me to jail for it. I don't care. It's Claudia's fault in the first place. There!" With the last word she drew a packet out of her sleeve and threw it on the table.

Alys picked up the little package of toilet paper and unwrapped it. Something like a piece of grayish yellow rock fell out.

"What—" began Alys, but then she stopped.

"I took it out of a glass case and chipped a bit off with his letter opener. I've ruined an archeological artifact. I'm a vandal and a thief. *And,*" she added as Alys drew her into her arms as if she were as young as Claudia, "I'm proud of it."

Charles was still gazing at the little chip of rock, perplexed. "What are you talking about? What did you do?"

"I vandalized the skull of an Aztec Indian. It was in a case in Dr. Foster's study." Janie pulled away from Alys and gestured at the piece of rock. "That's human bone."

It took Charles a moment to absorb this statement.

"But—bones are white. That thing's the wrong color."

"Idiot. It's hundreds of years old. Your bones aren't going to look so great in six hundred years either."

This struck Charles as exquisitely funny and he began to laugh, Alys and Claudia joining in. They laughed until they were exhausted, the tension of the last few minutes dissolving.

"Oh, Janie, you're so funny," said Claudia, and Janie flushed. No one had ever said such a thing to her before.

It was Alys who turned serious first. "We've got all the ingredients," she said, "and with Charles's money I can buy the equipment. Tomorrow afternoon we'll get ready. And tomorrow night, at moonrise, we'll make it."

chapter 8

THE MAKING OF
THE AMULET

No one was exactly sure when the moon would rise on Wednesday, so they all hurried that afternoon. Alys frantically hand-stitched four bags out of green silk bought at a fabric store. At four-thirty she placed the finished bags in her backpack, along with a small hammer, a needle and thread, a pair of scissors, and an Exacto knife. She then added the belt which Claudia had braided and a pair of blue bedroom slippers purchased from the five-and-dime. It had been cheaper to buy slippers than to dye regular shoes blue.

She, Charles, and Claudia were halfway out the door when she remembered the virgin garments.

"Drat! I've got virgin underwear and virgin socks," she

shouted to the others a few minutes later from behind her bedroom door, "and I suppose I can fit into the pink slacks Aunt Phyllis gave me last Christmas. But I'm darned if I can find a virgin shirt."

"I've got that T-shirt I bought in San Francisco," Charles offered. "The one Dad said I'm not allowed to wear on the street."

"Is it virgin? Did you try it on?"

"Never got the chance."

"Well, throw it in to me, then," said Alys. A moment later she gave a snort, and when she emerged she was wearing her jacket buttoned up to her chin. Charles took one look at her pants and began to laugh.

"So why do you think I've never worn them before? Come on, we're keeping Janie waiting."

At the old house Janie had the mortar and pestle on the kitchen table along with the gold crucible and the bottles.

"I've got everything ready," she said. "I'll read the ingredients to you. Those are awful pants."

"Thank you," said Alys. "Start reading."

As Janie unfolded the spell Alys removed her jacket and wound the braided red cord about her waist. She kicked off her shoes and put on the slippers. Then, clad in fuzzy blue bedroom slippers with pom-poms on the toes, pink pants a size too small, red belt, and Charles's black T-shirt with the indecent slogan, she took up the mortar and pestle.

In went the deadly nightshade, the wild elephant's ear, the bladderwort, and the stinking smut. Blobs of mercury slid over the powdered herbs as Alys poured quicksilver from the bottle. The minerals she pounded with the hammer before grinding them into the consistency of coarse sand. Then she dropped in a pinch of falcon's teeth, a handful of glittering sunfish scales, the flyclub, and a single phoenix feather snipped into pieces with the scissors. Finally, with a brief pause for ceremony, she pounded and ground the shard of human bone.

"Stir widdershins," said Janie, as she poured the mixture into the crucible. "Counterclockwise."

Alys stirred carefully, and presently the contents of the bowl resolved themselves into a multicolored mixture, mainly greenish brown because of the herbs, but with the brilliant glints of minerals through and through.

"Now for the blood and spit," she said and reached into her backpack.

"What," said Charles, "is *that?*"

"This," said Alys, "is an Exacto knife. Well, we need blood, don't we?" she added, as everyone stared at her.

"I was thinking of maybe a safety pin," Charles muttered.

"We can't sit here all night squeezing blood out of pinpricks. Come on, I've had first aid at the Y."

"So if you sever an artery you'll know how to apply a tourniquet?" But Charles allowed her to make a small jab at the tip of his finger. After an instant blood welled out.

"Drip into the bowl," instructed Alys, and she turned to prick Claudia. Claudia joined Charles over the crucible, and soon Alys was bleeding companionably along with them.

Janie hung back.

"It doesn't hurt—much," said Claudia.

There was a pause.

"I don't want to," said Janie.

"Get over here," said Alys impatiently. "You're not afraid of a little cut, are you?"

Janie's nostrils flared and she tightened her lips. But she held her position by the door.

"Look," said Charles. "You were practically willing to let Claudia sacrifice her whole finger, and now you're making a fuss about a few drops of blood. Coward!"

"Don't," said Alys. It was dark outside by now. "If she doesn't put her blood in, she can't go through the mirrors, that's all. We'll have to leave her here."

After another moment of deadly silence Janie yielded. Alys tried to be gentle, but somehow Janie's cut was deeper than the others', or else her blood was thinner, because finally her finger had to be wrapped in a dish-cloth to stop the bleeding. Janie was once again wearing her killer-frost expression by the time they had finished.

After they each spat into the bowl, Alys stirred again.

"And now we'd better go outside," she said. "We have to let the first ray of moonlight shine on the crucible."

"I don't suppose anyone noticed," said Janie in a polite, expressionless voice, "but it doesn't say the first ray of moonlight. It says the *reflection* of the first ray. As in mirror reflection."

"Hey, she's right," said Charles, checking the battered sheet of paper.

Alys wanted to shake Janie. "Couldn't you have mentioned this before?" she demanded angrily. "Instead of waiting until the last minute to show off how clever you are?"

Janie's purple eyes blazed. "There are dozens of mirrors in this place! We can use any one of them!"

"Any one small enough to carry. Claudia, run and find one while we take this stuff outdoors."

The grass was damp under Alys's slipper-shod feet as they walked out to the garden behind the house. Beyond this flat space the ground sloped steeply away, and the wood-covered hill stretched down to the lights of Villa Park below. They had barely reached the spot Alys had chosen when Claudia's voice came to them faintly.

"I can't get it out!" With the shout, Claudia herself appeared, flushed and panting. "I took the little mirror off the kitchen wall, but I can't get it through the door. It isn't heavy. It just—won't come out!"

It took Charles only a moment to ascertain that this was true. "It's like there's some kind of magic wall there," he said, returning. "Doesn't *anybody* have a mirror on them?"

Alys, in her sodden slippers and too-tight pants, clutched the crucible to her chest with one hand and juggled her backpack and the flashlight with the other. "Would we be standing here if we did?" she snapped, and then: "Oh, no—look." To the east a pale radiance showed in the sky, and a sliver of white appeared over the foothills.

There was instant pandemonium. "Where can we get a mirror?" "Nowhere—it's too late." "Could we use something else shiny?" "There isn't any time." "Janie, I'm going to *kill* you!"

"Wait!" shouted Charles. Half a crescent of white showed above the foothills as he fumbled with the zippered pocket of his windbreaker. Getting the pocket open at last, he pulled out a familiar flat shape—a Hershey bar.

"Charles," Alys screamed, purple-faced, "if all you can think about at this moment is your stomach—"

Charles tore off the outer paper wrapper in one motion, revealing the inner foil wrapper. "Here's your mirror," he said. "Or as good as. It'll reflect light."

The white crescent in the eastern sky looked elongated, as if its bottom horn clung to the hills below. Alys dropped her backpack and snatched the shining rectangle of foil from Charles, falling to her knees with the crucible in front of her.

"I don't know if this will work or not—I don't even know if I'm holding it right." Shakily, she shifted the foil back and forth, trying to judge the angle that would throw a ray on the crucible. The others crouched over her.

"Moonlight isn't like sunlight," said Charles. "I bet we won't even know exactly when it works."

He was wrong. On the word *works* the moon separated entirely from the mountains. At the same instant Alys saw the smudged foil blaze and then a beam of purest silver shot out to strike the golden crucible. There was a flash like summer lightning and Alys nearly fell backward. They were all blinded. When they could see again through the dazzling afterimage, the crucible was topped with a ghostly flame, translucent and radiant as the moonlight itself, rising twelve feet into the air.

"I wouldn't touch it if I were you," said Alys thickly, at last.

"*Touch* it!" Charles said, gaping.

They lost track of time, watching that cool, unearthly column of flame which neither rose nor fell but endlessly poured its energy upward. Long after they were too numb to feel the cold it began to flicker, and between one flicker and another it went dead. Blinking, the chilled watchers stirred.

In the crucible, the grayish, moisture-clotted mixture had undergone a transformation. It was now fine sand, the color of the eldritch flame, the color of moonlight, or running water, or the surface of an empty mirror. Janie, overcome by curiosity, tested it with one finger.

"Cool," she said huskily.

"Give me the bags," said Alys.

No one moved as Alys divided the star-colored sand into four parts and pinched it into the bags. No one spoke or urged her to hurry as she clumsily stitched the open ends of the bags closed. When it was done each of them took a bag and looked at it quietly, feeling the soft weight of the sand inside. And then they realized that it was all done and they were wet from kneeling on the grass and half-frozen from the night air and it was terribly late and they had to go home.

Stiffly, they gathered the used materials and started down the hill.

Above them, the crescent moon rose in the sky.

chapter 9

THE FIRST MIRROR

$I'll$ go first," said Alys gently.

"Let's get it over with, then," said Janie.

It was the next evening, just after moonrise, and they had been arguing all afternoon about which mirror to go through. Charles and Claudia wanted to try the cellar, maintaining that this was the logical place for a prisoner like Morgana to be kept, but Alys and Janie thought it would be more useful and less dangerous to use the little hallway between the kitchen and the living room, and as usual Alys had had the last word. Now she had also ended the debate about who would lead the way into the Wildworld.

She paused, looking at their four reflections in the hallway mirror and fingering the silk bag which hung from a shoestring at her neck. "Give me a moment after I go through," she said finally. "If there's something dangerous on the other side—like Cadal Forge—I'll come back fast."

She hesitated. "Everybody ready? Nobody has to go to the bathroom or anything?"

"Oh, let's hurry!" Claudia couldn't restrain herself any longer.

"Right," said Alys. She squared her shoulders and faced the mirror directly, one hand upraised as if to push aside a curtain of strung beads. She took a small step.

"Alys through the looking glass," said Charles, and he laughed nervously.

Janie leaned forward, and with all her strength, gave Alys a sudden shove in the middle of the back.

"Hey—"

"Look out!"

Charles grabbed for Alys but could not check her. She fell directly into the mirror, but instead of shards of glass and blood and breakage there was a kaleidoscopic blur of light. Charles saw an orange-red figure like the silhouette of a falling girl on a shifting blue-green background. Then the colors were gone, without even a ripple to show they had ever existed, and he was staring at his own open-mouthed reflection.

He rounded savagely on Janie. "What'd you *do* that for?"

Janie's purple eyes were fractionally wider than usual but she spoke calmly. "Just being helpful. I thought if I didn't she'd never do it by herself."

Charles and Claudia were too excited and amazed to stay angry. "Let's go in," said Claudia. "*I'm* going." She dove into the mirror as if she'd been doing it every day of her life. Again came the colors and the red-orange figure which passed through them.

When the glass cleared Charles and Janie looked at one another, then Charles put down his head and charged. He did not feel the surface of the mirror as he passed through it, but for an instant the air seemed to thicken and quiver around him. Then his foot came down and he found that he had stepped into a room he had never seen before. Alys and Claudia were staring about them in wonder.

"It worked," said Charles, looking at his own hands in surprise. His solid flesh had passed through solid glass.

"Here comes Janie!" cried Claudia, vastly excited.

Seeing someone come out of a mirror was even stranger than seeing someone go in. First the red-orange figure appeared and then Janie's disembodied leg swung out of it and then Janie herself was standing there.

"Doesn't it feel funny?" said Claudia with a delighted shiver.

Charles nodded. "Like electrified Jell-O."

"Shhh!" said Alys, looking around uneasily. They were still in a hallway, or corridor, but the ceiling was now twenty feet high and the floor and the walls were made of blocks of rough, pale limestone. Arches in those walls held massive wooden doors cross-barred with iron, and the whole scene was lit by torches which burned eerily blue without smoking.

"It's a castle," whispered Claudia, and Charles stepped over to a window set deeply in the wall. Through the panes of thickly glazed glass he could see moonlight falling on the inner courtyard.

"I don't see anyone out there," he whispered. "And I don't hear anything, either."

Everyone listened. The massive walls held silence as thick as butter. Only the flickering torches moved.

Alys let out her breath. "Maybe Cadal Forge isn't here," she said softly. "But we've got to be careful. All right, Charles, you and Claudia go to the dungeon—I mean the cellar. If you find Morgana, get her to the human side immediately, then come and tell us." This last instruction had cost Alys a great deal of heartache, but she had finally decided that Morgana's safety came before their own. "If you see anyone besides Morgana, run. Remember, *something got the vixen.*"

Charles nodded alertly, and he and Claudia moved stealthily away, through the nearest arch, toward the kitchen.

Janie was already testing a door which led out into the courtyard, and finding it locked.

"I wonder how many doors in this place are locked," she whispered.

"These aren't." Alys was standing in front of the enormous double doors which in their world shut off the living room from the hallway. They were so heavy that it took the combined weight of the two girls to move them.

"Oh . . ." breathed Alys as they stepped inside.

They were in the great hall of Fell Andred. As in the human house the ceiling was three stories high, but in the Wildworld the stories themselves were more lofty, and the ribs of the vaulted ceiling soared upward as if defying gravity. Thick columns sculpted like statues supported the galleries, and at the far end a staircase wound out of the northeast turret to end between two of these columns.

As they slowly walked the length of the hall Alys shrank from the titanic statues, which seemed to be staring down at them. Some merely looked impassive, but many had twisted smiles and an air of quietly waiting. . . .

"Here's a fire," said Janie.

The hearth was in proportion to the room, and in its cavernous depths a whole tree trunk was blazing. At a distance of ten feet the heat brought a flush to Alys's cheeks and tingled dryly against her outstretched palms. She stepped closer for a better look, and suddenly Janie grabbed her arm, pulling her out of the way as a fist-sized fireball burst out of the flames and shot toward her, flashing past with a sizzling sound. Gasping, she watched it careen off a wall and fly about the room until, with a hiss, it winked out and was gone.

"Thank you," said Alys when she could speak again. She added, "That makes up for pushing me through the mirror."

Janie looked quickly at her, then away. "Didn't think you realized that was me," she said. "Sorry."

"Forget it." Alys cast another glance around the hall, more uneasy than ever. That statue over there, of the man with steer's horns—hadn't it been on the other side before? And surely the winged woman above them hadn't been smiling so cruelly.

"I don't think Morgana is here," said Janie in a small voice.

"No," agreed Alys. There was nowhere to hide anyone. The vast room was bare except for the great dais which stood at the east end near the staircase and the glittering tapestries on the walls. It might have been a beautiful place, if one didn't mind the statues, of course, or that faint faraway music which disappeared when you tried to listen to it.

Yet right beside Alys, hanging in front of the fireplace, was something altogether lovely: a bird cage fashioned of twisted golden wires. "Look, Janie," she whispered, going on tiptoe to look into it. Then: "Oh!"

"What is it?" asked Janie, keeping well back in case it was something dangerous.

"It looks like . . . I think it's a snake." Somehow the thought of a snake being kept like a lovebird or canary was the most horrible of all. This is a different *world*, Alys thought, and all desire to explore left her. Aloud she said, "Anyway, it's dead."

"Well, good. Let's go over there, then." Janie nodded toward the dais, which stood in front of the largest mirror Alys had ever seen, a mirror large enough for four people to walk into abreast. But even as she spoke they heard another sound, barely audible above the crackle of the fire, a sound like a paper bag brushing across a wooden floor.

". . . if you please, gentle ladies . . ."

Alys stiffened. She looked up, down, around. She looked at Janie, who was doing the same thing.

". . . gentle ladies . . . if you please . . ."

"It's the snake," said Janie. There was a sort of horrified fascination in her face.

Alys put her head close to the cage. The snake was lying as still and quiet as before, but its black eyes glittered at her. It was alive.

". . . of your mercy, ladies . . . I beg you . . ." The voice was as dry and thin as a dead butterfly's wing.

"It's hurt," said Alys, somehow sure of this. "What's wrong? What can I do?" she said to the snake.

". . . if it would not be too much to ask . . . the heat . . . fire is death to my kind. . . ."

Now that Alys thought of it, she saw it would be madness to keep a bird or any other living creature so close to that great fire. She looked up and realized with dismay that the cage could not be detached from its chain. She would have to reach in and take the snake in her hands.

"Don't," said Janie.

Alys hesitated. She didn't want to do it, but she couldn't just walk away and leave the creature to die. "You won't—er, bite me, will you?"

"Ah, lady . . ." The tiny voice was so pained that Alys felt ashamed. With a sideways glance at Janie she unfastened the cage door and took out the snake, which was neither slimy nor scaly, but dry and very warm. It drooped limply from her hand, head and tail hanging like pieces of old string.

"It's cooler at the other end of the hall," said Janie. Janie might be difficult at times, but she never got hysterical and she seldom nagged. Alys felt grateful for this as she carried the snake back and laid it on the floor near the double doors.

"Is that any better?"

The snake gave a weak, appreciative wiggle. "My life . . . is yours. . . ."

"What was it doing there, anyway?" said Janie.

"Hush. It's tired out. It can't talk." Alys was tempted to pet the snake down its blue and coral length, but she resisted. Although it was nearly two feet long, its back was marred by little bumps or stubs, giving it the look of a very slim caterpillar.

"What were you doing in that cage?" said Janie again. "I just thought if Morgana did it we'd better know about it," she added, with a quelling look at Alys.

"The Lady Morgana . . . ah, no. It was that devil, Cadal Forge."

"Him!" said Alys. They strained to hear the papery voice.

"That cage was meant for a firebird, a phoenix . . . but he caught me and put me there lest I fly away."

"Fly?" said Janie.

"Like a butterfly," said Alys, pleased with her deductive powers. "You're a caterpillar, aren't you?"

When the creature spoke again its voice was a little stronger. "Gentle lady, you mock me." Then, with a laugh like a whispered sigh, it said, "Although only an infant of my kind, I am a Feathered Serpent."

"You mean you have wings?" Alys bent over the serpent, reaching a tentative finger toward one of the bumps. Now that she looked at them more closely, they didn't look decorative at all. They looked . . . like wounds. . . .

"Cadal Forge tore them off," whispered the serpent.

The stairway to the cellar was just off the kitchen, and it plunged narrow and straight into the darkness below. Moments after Charles and Claudia stepped onto it, the darkness engulfed them. Charles took a flashlight out of his windbreaker pocket and switched it on, but the light seemed pitifully weak, and illuminated only a small area of the steep, uneven stone steps. He put his free hand on the wall to steady himself and quickly snatched it back. The wall was *furry*—with slime, cobwebs, fungus, who knew what. He didn't turn the flashlight aside to see.

Behind him, Claudia had a firm grip on his windbreaker. Charles wanted to say something to reassure her, but the darkness and the silence closed his throat. It felt as if no one had spoken in this place for centuries.

They reached the bottom, cut off completely from the world of light and sound. The room was so large that it had the open-air feeling of a subterranean cavern walled with hewn stone and floored with hard-packed earth. With Claudia still clutching him desperately, Charles made the circuit of the room, keeping close to the bulk of the wall. If, he thought, something were to leap suddenly out of the blackness into the small bright spot the flashlight made . . .

When they got to the far end with its mirror of stained and battered steel, Charles began to feel a little better. Nothing had jumped out at them. But there was no sign of Morgana. Just to be sure, they would hug the other wall on the way back and look into the counterpart of Morgana's secret workroom, but he was already certain they would find nothing. This place was empty, deserted as a forgotten tomb. No one had disturbed its stillness for centuries.

It was then, of course, that a voice spoke out of the darkness behind them.

chapter 10

THE QUESTION GAME

The voice was slow and cold and thick, like frozen mud. It brought to mind all the long, cruel, inexorable processes of the earth, the erosion of mountains, the creeping of glaciers, the lazy drift of colliding continents. "Who . . . dares . . . trespass?" it said.

Charles and Claudia jerked around like marionettes on strings. The flashlight wavered hysterically around the room.

"What is it? Oh, what is it?" gasped Claudia.

"Who . . . dares . . . trespass?"

The light caught something moving. Charles focused on it, and promptly wished he hadn't. There was a *thing* out there in the darkness, a thing which seemed to be carved of moldering rock, and which was *swimming* through the ground as if the hard-packed earth were water. The thing had massive shoulders, knotted arms which scooped effortlessly through the soil, and a very large mouth. Claudia made a small noise and subsided.

"Who—what are you?" croaked Charles.

"Did you not come seeking the Groundsler?"

"The . . . Groundsler?" Charles swallowed. The thing was between them and the stairway.

"What manner of Weerul sprite are you?" the creature continued, moving closer yet.

"I'm not a sprite. I'm a human. Are you—"

"Ha!" The single word exploded around them. "Once again I have won the game. Still, you were such poor opponents, my dears, that there is little glory in it."

"What are you talking about? What game?" Charles broke off with an exclamation. For an instant he'd had the feeling he was sinking—he *was* sinking. Turning the flashlight on his own feet he saw, to his horror, that the earth and rock were flowing around them like molasses. Before he could cry out, his feet were embedded in it up to the ankles.

"Charles?" Claudia's voice came to him quietly. "Charles, I'm stuck."

"So . . . am I, Claude." He looked up, fear now mingling with anger. "What do you think you're doing? Let us go!"

"Go? Foolish child, you've lost."

"Lost *what?*"

"The Question Game, of course. I am the Groundsler, the One Who Questions. You gave me an answer, and so you lost. Now I will give you my answer, which is to say I will eat you." It chuckled at its little joke, with a sound like a tar pit bubbling.

"We answered a question—so you *eat* us?"

"That is the game. And a very good game, too. It's been a long time since I've had company. Though a minor sorcerer did stumble down here the other day, looking for a shovel. He was delicious," the Groundsler added reminiscently.

"I want Alys," said Claudia. "Alys! Alys!"

"Not like that, Claude, they won't hear you. Let's do it together. One, two, three: Alys! Alys! Janie!"

"Oh, by all means," said the Groundsler, settling deeper into the rock. "I'm anxious to meet all your little friends."

Alys and Janie were far above in the castle where no human ears could hear the disturbance below. Alys was at that moment staring at the serpent with a sick feeling in her stomach and a metallic taste in her mouth.

"We're going to get him," she said, hardly knowing her own voice. "We're going to get Cadal Forge. I promise."

"Lady, you must not distress yourself so. . . . I am of no great value. . . ." The serpent's voice was fading.

"We were going to do it anyway." She sounded abrupt and ungracious, but Alys knew Janie meant well. "Is he here in the castle now?"

"I think . . . not. . . . I have not seen him for days. . . ."

"What can we do to help you?" said Alys gently.

"There is . . . a grotto in the conservatory . . . where I might lie until I heal. My wings will not grow back . . . but I will live without them." The serpent dropped its head to the floor, then lifted it weakly. "Pardon, good ladies, my saviors, but is either of you the Lady Alys? Or the Lady Janie?"

"We're both," said Alys, confused. "I mean, I'm Alys. How did you know?"

"Two voices below call your names."

"Charles and Claudia—oh, no!" Alys sprang up.

"Wait, good my ladies, wait—"

But Alys was already out the door, with Janie at her heels. The serpent lay still a moment gathering its vanished strength. Then, painfully, as slowly as a flower turning toward the sun, it began to drag itself after them.

Alys nearly broke her neck on the first step in her mad rush to get down to the cellar.

"Charles? Claudia? Where are you?"

"Alys!" Charles's voice came from far below her, echoing. "Alys, *don't say anything! Don't talk!"*

"What? What do you mean? Are you all right?"

"Yes! I mean, no! Listen, Alys, just shut up! Don't either of you say anything until I finish explaining! All right? All right." Charles's voice became businesslike. "There's a—a thing down here called a Groundsler. It's got Claudia and me. *But it can't get you unless you answer a question.* Get it? It's going to ask you questions, and if you answer it, it wins. If it answers you, you win. You can say anything you want, but it has to be a question. Understand?"

Alys had reached the bottom of the steps and now she stood still, dumbfounded. Had to be a question?

Behind her Janie's voice was clear and icily calm.

"What happens when it loses?"

"It has to do whatever you tell it. If you win it'll let us go. I—I can't see any other way to get out."

"Where is it now?"

"Where else would I be, my dear?" The head surfaced a few feet in front of them, breaking through the solid earth. Pale eyes gleamed like minerals in the single shaft of light. Alys started to scream, choked, and stumbled back, wondering dizzily if a scream was a question or not.

Janie stepped to her side, and spoke carefully. On her face was the dispassionate, preoccupied look she wore when playing a difficult game of chess. "Alys, do you understand the rules?"

"I . . . er . . . I . . . can sort of . . . uh, I do— don't I?" Alys threw her hands up helplessly and pressed her lips together. She was out of her depth.

Janie nodded, and turned to the creature. "Are you the Groundsler?" she asked.

"My dear, upon whose domain do you intrude?" The slow, terrible voice sounded amused.

"What are you doing with Charles and Claudia?"

There was a muddy chuckle. "Isn't it obvious?"

"I think it's going to—eat us," called Charles. "That is, if you don't win. But you will," he added hastily.

Janie thought a moment, then addressed the creature. "Do you know Morgana, the sorceress who built this castle?"

The Groundsler moved lazily. "Who does not know the Mirror Mistress?"

"Are you in league with Cadal Forge?"

"Do you seek to insult me?"

"Do you know where Morgana is now?"

"What makes you ask?"

83

Janie hesitated, unable to think of a way to respond to this without making a statement. The Groundsler, which had so far been content to let her take the lead, suddenly switched to the offensive.

"Did you not know the risk you took, coming to this place?"

"Er—which place: the cellar or the castle?"

"Or the world?" Alys put in suddenly. She then retreated in confusion. The Groundsler moved forward, and now the questions came quickly.

"What part of the human world do you come from, my dear?"

"Why should I tell you?"

"And how did you get here?"

"What do you think the mirrors are for?"

"And what is your business with Cadal Forge?"

"That's none of *your* business—uh, is it?"

It had her on the run now.

"What is your name, little one?"

"Didn't you hear the others shouting it?"

"I wonder, shall I be eating Janie or Alys first?"

"Don't you . . . ah, think it may be unwise, eating *any* friends of Morgana's?"

"Will the sorceress, then, come to your aid?"

"What do you think?"

"What do *you* think?"

Janie was stung. "Hey—is repeating fair?"

"Yes," said the Groundsler.

There was a moment of utter silence. Then Alys gave a wild triumphant yell and grabbed Janie around the neck.

"We won! We won! I mean—we won, didn't we?" Just in case, she tried to turn it into a question.

The Groundsler was standing—or wading, or whatever —as still as the rock it appeared to be made of.

"Impossible," it said at last. It sounded shaken.

"Let us go!" bellowed Claudia. "You promised!"

"Promised what?" said the Groundsler sullenly.

"Oh, no you don't," said Janie. "I won, and I'm telling you to let them go."

The Groundsler made a noise like a volcano and a noise like a glacier and a noise like a gravel pit collapsing. Around Charles's and Claudia's ankles the rock liquefied and melted away. They were free.

No one ever moved faster than they did getting back up the stairs. Safe in the kitchen at last, they were all talking at once as they moved toward the hallway mirror.

"What's that?" Charles pulled up short, staring at what looked like a length of blue cord on the hallway floor.

"Oh, the serpent! Don't stomp it, Charles!"

Charles, who had had no idea of stomping it, withdrew indignantly. Alys dropped to her knees.

"You shouldn't have tried to move," she said.

"Gentle mistress . . . I came to . . ." The voice faded.

"It said 'to warn us,'" said Janie.

Alys was touched. "Oh . . . oh, thank you. But what can we do for you, now?"

Out of the faint hiss that followed only two words were distinguishable: *conservatory* and *grotto*. Weakly, the serpent guided them back into the great hall and through a little doorway in the wall opposite the hearth.

The conservatory was a tangle of weeds and briars,

with narrow paths half-buried under twining vegetation. Behind this, like a small natural cave, was the grotto.

Alys and the others stopped in their tracks.

One wall was ruined, and moonlight and chill outdoor air flooded in. But the other walls! They were encrusted with minerals of every hue. Rose quartz crystals like pink diamonds, spiky red cinnabar, forest green malachite, translucent gypsum, and, yes, red wulfenite, hornblende, and peacock coal were clustered side by side with topaz, tourmaline, amethyst, garnet, and opal.

But if the walls were a rainbow, the floor was like a dream. Ankle-deep, and in some places knee-deep, it was piled with treasure. There were pitchers and drinking bowls and goblets, all gleaming with the soft heavy yellow light of solid gold. There were ropes of pearls and heaps of necklaces, armlets, brooches, and diadems. There were gem-encrusted chalices, and golden candlesticks and sceptres.

"People bring them to me," explained the serpent simply, as they stood agape. "They have, ever since I hatched here. It is . . . traditional, when the Council sends a serpent's egg . . . to bring gifts. . . ."

Gently, Alys set the little creature among the piles. "The Weerul Council sent you?"

"Every great house has its serpent guardian. But I have failed . . . failed both the Council and my lady. . . ."

A tiny hope which had sprung up in Alys's mind died. "You don't know where Cadal Forge imprisoned Morgana."

"He seized me first. . . . I knew nothing, lying before that terrible fire." The serpent sagged in defeat and exhaustion. "I cannot help you with that. But"—it looked up at her pleadingly—"there is something I can give you. Choose what you will from my treasures. All I have is yours for the asking. . . ."

Alys shook her head, but the others lost no time in offering suggestions. Charles proffered a crown set with walnut-sized raw rubies, Janie tenderly dusted off an exquisitely enameled vase, and Claudia dived into a pile headfirst and emerged with what looked like a pair of silver-plated thumbscrews.

But Alys, when she at last realized the serpent was serious, put her hand immediately on the only weapon to be seen in the hoard, a dagger in a stained and battered leather sheath. It nestled into her hand.

"Not *that*," said Charles. "It's hideous."

Alys drew the blade.

It shimmered like liquid light in her hand, putting all the other treasures to shame. The sides were very slightly scalloped, with thin diagonal lines running between the scallops, shining bright and pale on the pearlescent background.

"It is a gannelin dagger," said the serpent quietly. "Made in the Golden Age. There are only three others like it in Findahl." Utterly depleted by this speech, it sagged down among the piles. "Good-bye, my lady Alys," it whispered faintly, burrowing into a pile of loose gems. A moment later it had disappeared and there was only a distant hiss of "Thrown or wielded, it will not easily miss its mark. . . ."

Alys sheathed the dagger again, concealing its brightness, and thrust it into her belt. She was suddenly very tired.

"Come on," she said. "Let's go home."

chapter 11

SHADOWS ON
THE WALL

I join the shadows on the wall / To watch with weary silver eyes / Poets who soliloquize . . ."

"Janie, don't be morbid," said Alys.

". . . About the fate that awaits us all," Janie finished in a whisper. She was regarding herself in the study mirror, which was so dark and tarnished that it reflected only a dim and cloudy outline of a girl back at her. Having finished the poem, she bit into the sandwich Alys had packed for her. It was nearly nine o'clock on Friday night, and they were waiting for moonrise. They waited in the study because from this window they had a clear view of the driveway—and of any local law enforcement officers who might be coming up it.

"What I'm worried about," said Alys, "is locked doors. For every locked door we find in the Wildworld, that means one more trip through a mirror. And we're running out of *time*."

This started up the old argument about whether or not they should separate in the Wildworld in an attempt to cover the castle four times as fast. Alys had just stated categorically that from now on they all traveled together, with her going first, when Janie did it.

She had been staring into the dark mirror with disfavor since they all sat down, and now she picked up a crumpled napkin and began to rub at the tarnish. This polishing had no discernible effect on the dirt, but as her hand slipped and her finger touched the surface of the mirror there was a blue-green shimmer, a vermilion silhouette, and then there were only three people in the room.

"The moon must have risen!" cried Charles, jumping to his feet. "And she was wearing the amulet!"

Alys spoke through clenched teeth. "She'd better come back," she said, and then, several minutes later, "She'd better have a good reason for not coming back."

"We'll have to go after her," said Charles. They had planned on going through the kitchen mirror and exploring the west wing.

A tense second or two later Alys agreed, and very gingerly she touched the grimy mirror.

She emerged in a room lit by a single great candle on a tall standing candlestick. The light flickered strangely, but it was sufficient to show her that she was entirely alone. Moreover, as she began to move toward the closed door to search for Janie, she found that she *liked* being alone, that she had no particular desire to find her sister or anyone else. She felt strangely light and free. She wanted . . . oh, she wanted to slip into some dark and lonely place and stay there forever, watching.

"Alyssss . . ." The voice was eerie, and seemed to come from a long distance, like the music in Morgana's great hall. "Alys, come heeeeere. . . ."

Alarm cut through the pleasantly forlorn feeling. She turned around and around, but the room was empty of all but flickering candlelight and dancing shadows. Her hand went to the gannelin dagger which hung at her belt, but the feel of it was dull. She began to think about dark places again.

"Alys, it's meeeee. . . ."

The shock, when it came, was terrible. As she turned, searching, she found herself looking into the mirror, which in this world was bright and untarnished. It reflected her, alert and wary, and behind her . . . unmistakably . . . Charles, Claudia, and Janie.

Wildly she spun around, looking back and forth from the mirror to the empty air behind her, and noticing that the three other reflections were doing this also. The room was filled with ghostly voices.

"I can't believe this—" "Where *are* you all?" "Interesting, isn't it?" "Alys!"

The empty air, she realized gradually, was not empty. If she looked hard she could just discern three vague forms in the moonlight, forms apparently made of very thin darkness.

"We're ghosts," said the smallest form, lifting insubstantial arms in despair. "Oh, Alys, I don't *like* it."

Distant laughter sounded in Alys's ear. "Not ghosts,"

said Janie's voice. "Shadows. And what I don't like is this candlelight. Too bright. Let's get out of it."

"But how do we stop being shadows?" wailed Claudia.

"It's all right," sighed Janie. "I should think it would be obvious. If we *want* to change, we go through this mirror where we can see ourselves the way we used to be."

"We'd have to open the window shutter first and let the moonlight in." Charles's wraithlike form seemed to shudder at the thought.

"We'll worry about it later," said Alys. The truth was that she had no desire to stop being a shadow. For the first time since meeting the vixen she felt unburdened, absolved of all responsibility. It was a very pleasant feeling, as if no one in the world was real except her. Right now she wanted to find someplace dark, and quiet, and faraway.

But when she tried to take hold of the door handle to open the door she found she could not move it.

"We're incorporeal," murmured Janie. "Bodiless. We can touch each other but not anything else, not anything solid."

They could not move the shutter either. Janie thought they should be able to drift *through* solid matter if they willed it hard enough, but no one could manage this.

There were several moments of silence.

"So what do we do now?" said Charles at last, not as if he cared much.

"Nothing," said Alys calmly. "There's nothing at all for us to do."

Janie and Charles accepted this without surprise. They settled back against a wall, content simply to wait . . . and watch. Only Claudia whimpered a little.

"Hush," said Alys distantly. Nothing seemed very real.
Then Charles said, "Listen."

They all heard it—a snuffling, scratching noise in the
hall outside. The next instant the door burst open.

It struck Alys on the forehead and shoulder, but the
blow was softened as she seemed to melt into the wood.
Her shadow-indifference was shattered. She fell backward
as much from surprise and horror at the sight of the animal on the threshold as from the impact.

Cats . . . she had never liked cats. And this was some
unnatural combination of leopard and basilisk, with feline head and hindquarters and reptilian snout and claws.
Its shoulders were covered by heavy, armored scales
which looked almost metallic. It could not see or smell
her, she realized, as the unblinking yellow eyes stared
right through her, but it could hear her panting breath.

"Move away from it," hissed Charles, from his kneeling
position behind the door. The great head swung toward
him immediately, distracted, and from the scaly throat
came a whining sound. Trembling, trying not to breathe,
Alys inched backward into the safety of the veiling darkness.

An icy hand touched hers, although here she could see
no form at all. "Please, let's go home," whispered Claudia.

The animal turned at even this faint sound, the whine
becoming a high snarl of frustration.

"Briony," said a man's voice in the hall, "what is it?"

Alys's heart leapt into her throat. Everything was all
too real now, terrifyingly real. But there was no time to
think or move, because he was *there*, framed in the doorway, with the monster-cat turning to fawn on him. He

was human, or at least he was a man, but there was a strange similarity of movement between him and the animal, a sinuous, stalking grace. After one long look Alys knew she would much rather face the Groundsler.

"Yes," said the man, rubbing the cat's hideous head as he gazed around the room. "I feel it, too. Something amiss." He stepped forward and the candlelight played on his face. It was not a bad face, handsome even, until a trick of the light deepened the shadows of lines around the mouth and showed the tightness of skin under the hooded eyes. There was weariness there, thought Alys, and driven purpose, and cruelty.

The next moment the light changed and showed only a tall man with a cropped helmet of dark hair and a remote, abstracted expression. He wore a vaguely military outfit of dark red tunic and leggings. Although his eyes still looked about the room, his gaze seemed turned inward now, upon some distant scene of pain and amusement.

Even as he stood there, a second man, younger than he, more tired, less assured, stepped into the doorway. This one was garbed in flowing gray robes which gave him a clerical air. Yet despite his youth and tiredness and monkish demeanor, he and the other man had something in common: power. It emanated from them in waves so strong that Alys could almost see it.

"Cadal?" the young man said quietly. "Cadal, we've got her."

For a long moment Cadal Forge stood unmoving, apparently heedless. At last, he stirred and sighed. Without turning, he said, "That's good, Aric. Bring her to me."

Aric glanced about the dark and barren room. "Here?"

Cadal Forge nodded, already gone in reverie again, his absent yes barely audible.

As the younger sorcerer departed, leaving the door ajar, Alys felt Janie's panicked hand on her shoulder. "Let's *go*," hissed Janie's voice in her ear.

"Be quiet," Alys breathed, for Briony was straining forward, whimpering. "I have to see what happens. It could be Morgana they've got."

"I don't care *who* it is," whispered Janie between set teeth, but Alys dragged her farther back into the darkness, and they joined the shadows on the wall as Aric returned.

He was escorting a girl, a very young and delicate-looking girl, who wore a simple white garment, like a Greek chiton, girdled with ribbon. A gold band encircled her hair, which was straight and fine and the color of moonlight. In her right hand she held a bunch of purple loosestrife, still dripping wet; on her left wrist perched a small bright-eyed falcon. The whole room seemed lighter for her presence, and the four shadows shrank back even farther, feeling exposed.

"Hello there," said the girl, offering Cadal Forge the loosestrife.

"Oh, leave your rubbish!" cried Aric, slapping the bouquet from her hands.

"Softly, Aric, softly," said Cadal Forge. With complete gravity he bent and retrieved the flowers, then returned them to the girl. "So you have been gathering blossoms near the marsh, have you, and playing by the water?" His words were courteous, his manner charming, but it was clear that he was speaking as a great king speaks to a half-witted child.

"Well, I have a new amusement for you," he added, and for just an instant the force of personality, the commanding strength that lay under his mockery, was apparent. Then he smiled, and his voice was almost lilting as he said, "Come, you enjoyed our last venture together."

The girl laughed musically with him, then stopped. "Yes," she said, sobering, "but, you see, I'm busy now. I've just caught this sweet thing in my Wood." And she pursed her lips to the falcon, which hissed viciously. Its talons gripped her wrist cruelly, but she showed no sign of pain or distress.

"Very sweet," said Cadal Forge dryly. "But what I ask will take your mind off him only for a few moments. Listen to me, Elwyn. You were glad enough to listen before and make mischief for your shrewish sister."

What he said next was lost on Alys. So this was Elwyn Silverhair, Morgana's Quislai half sister! This was the person responsible for putting the entire human world in danger, the person who had outwitted the Mirror Mistress and opened the doors for the enslavement of Earth. . . .

"But I don't *want* to play anymore," said Elwyn, stamping one small bare foot petulantly. "I already did what you asked me to."

"Yes, you brought me Morgana. But you neglected to bring that slinking familiar of hers, and I was forced to run it down myself. And while it was loose I believe—I have reason to suspect—that it taught others the secret of the mirrors. What I want of you, Elwyn, is to cross to the Stillworld once more and find out the truth of this. If I am about to have human visitors here I would like to . . . to prepare some suitable greeting for them."

In the darkness, Claudia buried her head in Alys's shadowy lap.

"But I've already told you I'm busy." Elwyn put her head on one side and smiled at him ingenuously. "You see, there are reed whistles to make, and flowers to gather, and I want to fly my falcon and see her bring down other birds. . . ."

"I am aware of the many pressing demands on your time," said Cadal Forge. "But for the sake of our long friendship, surely you can spare an hour. I really must insist."

The way he said it, Alys could not imagine anyone daring to refuse. But—

"No," said Elwyn flatly, dropping the smile and shaking her silvery head for emphasis. "I've made up my mind, Cadal Forge, and I don't wish to argue. I will not go."

"Then you will *stay*," cried the sorcerer, suddenly unrecognizable with fury. Strangely, his hooded eyes hardly seemed to see Elwyn, but rather stared blindly through her. "You will remain a prisoner in this house until you obey me!"

"And how will you keep me? I see no thornbranches here."

"You see a Red Staff." Something passed, blindingly fast, from Aric's hands to those of the master sorcerer. It was a length of wood like a quarterstaff, dull red in color. The head was carved in the hideous semblance of a griffin, and as Cadal Forge pointed the staff at Elwyn, long twisted branches, laden with thorns, shot out from the griffin's mouth.

With a ringing laugh, Elwyn danced lightly out of the way, and in a single movement reached the window. No one saw how the shutter came open, but it did. Placing her hands on the sill, she swung herself lithely through it. Her sweet laughter hung mockingly on the air for a moment and was gone.

Aric sprang to the window and leaned out. "We must stop her!" he cried. "If she speaks of this—"

"No, no. Let be," said Cadal Forge. The savage passion had left him. He passed a hand over his forehead, blinking, and seemed to withdraw. "She will have forgotten it within the hour," he added, as Aric still looked out.

Reluctantly, the younger sorcerer turned, closing the wooden shutter once more. "She was our only hope of finding what lies beyond the mirrors," he said dully.

Cadal Forge had recovered himself, and a faint smile touched his lips. "No," he said. "I suspected it would come to this. And there is another, more intelligent and reliable ally at hand."

"Who?"

"Thia Pendriel."

Aric stared at him as if he had gone mad. When he spoke at last, it was in the flat voice of unbelief. "Thia Pendriel. Silver Guildmistress and a magistrate of the Council. Originator of the Plan of Separation. Thia Pendriel, who ordered you executed for treason, who herself helped to cast the portal which placed you in a Chaotic Zone to die—"

"And thus was unwittingly responsible for what I found in that Zone." Reaching into the folds of material at his breast, the sorcerer drew out a fist-sized jewel, a ruby, irregularly shaped but so clear it looked like a chunk of red ice. He weighed it in his hand as he continued speaking. "Thia Pendriel, who hates Morgana for winning the

Gold Staff away from her in her youth more than she ever hated me. Thia Pendriel, who has skills surpassing all others' at bringing far-distant scenes to light, and who can turn the mirrors themselves into windows so that we may see the other side."

Aric was still shaking his head as if stunned. "But should the Council learn of the Society's existence—"

"They will not learn of it from her," said Cadal Forge. Once again his expression was thoughtful, remote. "There is much you do not understand, Aric. Thia Pendriel has made a study of the mirrors; she knows all there is to know about them—except what no one but Elwyn could tell her, that on the night of the solstice they open to all. And this last secret she will pay dearly to learn. She is interested in the Stillworld for her own reasons."

"Which we do not know."

"Nor does she know ours," murmured Cadal Forge. The dreaming look enfolded him as he stared into the darkness and smiled.

Aric looked at him in uneasy surprise. "But she *must* know ours, if she is to aid us. And I daresay she must have her share of the Stillworld as well—"

"Yes, yes, whatever her price is we must meet it." Cadal Forge had refocused with a start. Now he turned to Aric and examined him. "You still do not agree. What are you afraid of? Perhaps"—he straightened, his shadow lengthening on the far wall—"you think I cannot match her power."

The younger man turned the color of old cheese, and averted his eyes. "No, my lord," he whispered after a long silence. "I know what you have found, and how you use it."

"Then let me save it for the humans, and don't tempt me to use it on *you*," said the other, relaxing, and smiling again. "My old friend, be at ease," he added gently. "The councillor and I have met secretly more than once since my 'execution,' and I know her weaknesses. I leave for Weerien tomorrow." He moved to lay a hand on the shoulder of Aric, who still looked slightly sick—and stopped cold. Alys had been so mesmerized by the conversation that she had left her shelter in the darkness and crept forward, by degrees, to hear better. At last, without realizing it, she had come into the line of sight of the mirror, and as Cadal Forge stepped forward he suddenly found himself gazing at the reflection of a very material young woman.

Their gazes locked in the mirror and Alys felt the force of those crystal gray eyes like a blast of heat from a furnace. With a gasp, she flung herself down into the shadows, and her reflection disappeared from the bright glass.

"What sorcery is this?" cried Aric, but it was Cadal Forge who whirled around swift as thought, his keen eyes razing the exact spot where Alys and the other three lay trembling. Yet even those eyes could see nothing, for shortly he turned back to his associate.

"I cannot tell," he said, and several times as he spoke he looked from the mirror to the wall, and back again. "But you must bring the Gray Staff and work a spell to reveal all that is hidden in this room. And I . . . I must cast a portal to Weerien at once. Our need of Thia Pendriel is greater than I thought."

Aric nodded and hurried from the room. But Cadal Forge, despite his words, hesitated, looking meditatively into the shadows. By his side Briony crooned deep in her throat, her yellow eyes fixed on Elwyn's hawk, which had not escaped with its mistress, but perched uneasily on a ledge in the rafters.

At the continued sound the sorcerer looked up, following her gaze. Then, with an abstracted glance at his familiar, he lightly laid the fingers of one hand across the Red Staff. The hawk, which had taken flight in fear, suddenly thrashed and plummeted to the stone floor, one wing broken.

Alys covered Claudia's eyes with a shadowy hand as Briony pounced.

"Are you truly beyond the mirrors, friends of Morgana? Are you indeed watching? Then see this." Cadal Forge spoke above the noises Briony made with the hawk. Once again he brought out the great jewel, holding it in sight of both mirror and shadows. "Behold Heart of Valor, a jewel from the time of Unmaking, recreated again—by me. Shall I tell you how I did it?" The sorcerer spoke casually, as if addressing honored guests he could see. In fact all at once he seemed to be enjoying himself.

"When the Council cast me into the Chaotic Zone my faithful Aric managed secretly to send me my staff. Even with all the power of the Red I struggled—I nearly succumbed to the maelstrom. But my will to live was strong. I wrestled with that great Zone as if it were an enemy that could be conquered—and I did conquer. I woke from deathlike sleep to find desolation all around me, but no Chaos. All was quiet. Natural law had been restored. But on the ground before me lay a jewel. I recognized it as one of the *bas imdril*, one of the Gems of Power which the Council Unmade long ago, and which I, in my struggles, had somehow created again. And which I have mastered

—so." The sorcerer fit the great Gem into his staff, and the griffin seemed crowned with fire. "Not even the Council knows of its existence, or that, with a word, I can do *this.*" The ruby traced a wide circle in the air, and, as the sorcerer murmured intently, the circle became a cylinder, a tunnel of shimmering light stretching off to infinity.

"I defy you to oppose me," said Cadal Forge quietly, and he stepped into the portal of light. It shrank and closed behind him, and the room was left to darkness and the flickering of the candle.

A dim figure took shape before that candle as Charles jumped from the shadows. "Hurry!" he said. "Before Aric gets back!"

"Hurry where?" whispered Janie.

Aric had reclosed the shutter and the door. There was no moonlight, and no escape.

Charles tried futilely to wrench the shutter open before turning back.

"We've got to do *something*—"

"We *can't,*" said Janie. Then she suddenly began to laugh. "We can't do anything. We're absolutely helpless!"

"Stop it," said Alys. "Janie, be quiet!"

Alys herself was sick with fear, not the least because Briony had finished with the hawk and was now turning languid yellow eyes toward the sound of their voices. If they were truly shadows, those steely claws could not hurt them, but as it was . . .

"He's coming back!" cried Charles from the door.

Flattened against the wall, with Briony sniffing at her feet and Claudia sobbing convulsively beneath her arm, Alys tried to think. If only they were truly shadows—but

Janie had said they *ought* to be, that they just weren't willing it hard enough.

She thrust Claudia away from her and sprang to stand before the closed shutter. "Briony! You hideous old lizard, come here!"

"Alys!"

"Charles, if this doesn't work out for me, you get the others back! At least you'll have moonlight. Here I am, kitty! You want me, don't you? Come on. Come for me, you *snake!*" She drew the gannelin dagger, and alone of all her possessions it shone out brightly, etched against the shadows. Footsteps sounded in the hall. Briony crouched low, snarling, her eyes fixed on the dagger. "Come for me, girl!"

With a blood-chilling yowl the beast leapt for her throat and Alys closed her eyes and thought for all she was worth about shadows, about vapor, mist, and ether. The savage yowl shrilled into a cry of surprise as Briony passed right through her and crashed with a terrible impact into the shutter. With a tearing sound the ancient wood gave way and the sorcerer's familiar, unable to stop herself, went with it. Unlike Elwyn's laughter, the scream emitted by Briony did not hang on the air, but went down and down and down.

"Now!" cried Alys, moonlight pouring in the shattered window. As they plunged toward the mirror she saw Aric reflected behind them, and saw that he saw their reflections and had the Gray Staff outstretched, his face twisted with fury as he mouthed words. Then, with a final bound, she reached the Passage and the air blazed turquoise blue around her.

chapter 12

THE THIRD MIRROR

That same night, in the Wildworld, in a room which had been stripped of anything she might find useful, Morgana Shee leaned her head wearily against the sorcerous bars in the window.

It had been twelve days since her capture, and she still could not understand what Cadal Forge wanted.

She had known his mother, a lady of one of the great houses of Findahl. And she had known *him*, child, youth, and man. She had watched him win a Red Staff at an unprecedentedly young age and listened, with delight, as he then adroitly argued his way out of the traditional apprenticeship in Weerien. When he set himself up in a city-state of the Stillworld called Florence, and began to study with a human master, she had visited him often.

She remembered the last time she had seen him there,

when he had showed her—oh, with what enthusiasm!—
his chemical compounds and reagents and his newest
treatise on the nature of matter. She had admired them—
and then she had begged him to go to one of the Eastern
countries where witchcraft was not a crime, or at least to
come with her to England, where the Inquisition held less
sway.

He had laughed at her, handsome in his loose silk shirt
and fur-trimmed jerkin.

"I'm tired of wandering. Besides, how can I leave Firenze? My teacher, Signore Gallura, is here."

"And his daughter, also?"

"Ah . . ." He had smiled sideways at her. "So you've
seen Celeste. Well, they are both here, and I can leave
neither of them."

"Oh, my friend, you are so young. . . . Stay, then, but
be on guard. What your teacher teaches is not orthodox,
and *that*"—the treatise—"is close to heresy. If you need
my help, send your cousin Terzian to me in England."
And she had left him.

Terzian had come less than a year later, not by portal,
for the White Staff had not the power to cast one, but
over land and sea. By the time she reached Morgana,
Cadal had been in the hands of the Inquisition for a
month.

"And they will burn him soon, for they are afraid of
him," the young sorceress had said, shuddering, as Morgana made frantic preparations for the journey.

"They should be afraid! The wielder of a Red Staff—
how could they even hold him?"

Terzian shook her head. "When they summoned
Signore Gallura for questioning my cousin went, too, but

he did not take his staff. Instead he took his notebooks and his drawings. He was convinced that even the Inquisitors could be swayed by reason, that he could make them understand that science is no heresy, no evil."

"Oh, Cadal!"

"When they showed the signore the instruments of torture, he fell to his knees and wept. He recanted all he'd taught or written contrary to doctrine, and he said that he was not a heretic but that Cadal was a sorcerer. If he'd known how right he was he never would have dared say it."

Morgana had arrived in Florence barely in time to snatch the young sorcerer from the very heart of the flames. She had known, as she cast a protective sphere around him and bore him away, that he had been terribly injured, but only back in the Wildworld, at Fell Valdris, the castle of Terzian's father, did she see the extent of what the humans had done.

Although his joints healed, and his hands, and the flesh they had bruised and burned and bled, his mind remained in darkness. He would listen to no excuses on behalf of the Stillfolk he had so recently loved, and when she tried to give him comfort he repulsed her.

"You don't know," he'd said, his gray eyes burning like coals in a thin and ravaged face. "You have no conception of what they can do—yes, what feeble, short-lived humans can do to the wielder of a Red Staff! With it I could have killed them with a word, a gesture. . . ." He turned away and his voice sank to a whisper. "Instead, I prayed to die."

"Cadal, I understand—"

"You do not *understand*. How could you, you—*Quis-lai*."

She returned to England without speaking to him again. Yet, three months later, when Terzian appeared at her gates with the news that he had been imprisoned by the Council, she did not hesitate.

"I do not ask you for help this time," his cousin said in a low voice as Morgana cast a portal to Avalon Passage, "but I thought it your right to know. As for me, I renounce him. If he had killed only the man . . . but not the household and the servants! The daughter was only a child."

"A human child," said Morgana. She was terribly afraid of what it might have done to Cadal himself, to awaken from the daze of maddened fury and find Celeste's blood on his hands. For he had truly loved the girl.

The Council had merely taken his staff and confined him to a room at Fell Valdris. His uncle Calain said that Cadal had not slept or eaten since arriving there, and when Morgana entered the room she found him sitting far from the candlelight, his head so low she could not see his face.

A tremor seemed to go through him as she entered, but he would not rise or look at her. And Morgana's heart had been torn by pity.

"You must not sit here in the dark," she said. "And you must listen to your uncle, and eat." She sighed and shut her eyes and tried to think what to do next.

When he finally spoke his voice was so hoarse and indistinct that she had to step closer to hear him.

"At the end," he said, "she begged for mercy. She wept

and said I was far more terrible than the Inquisition. . . ."

Morgana winced and turned away, then turned back and laid her hand on his shoulder. "Cadal. I know. You must try to forget."

It was only then, bending close to comfort him, that she saw that he was smiling.

She had spoken but a single sentence to Calain, who waited outside the door: "If the Council does not lock him up, I advise you to do it." She had returned to England only to find nothing was fresh or fair there anymore, and had begun to think seriously about moving to the New World.

And still she could scarcely credit that he was doing what he was doing now. Intrigues against the Council, yes, that she understood, but this madness . . .

Madness, yes! For when had Cadal Forge's ambition ever run to sovereignty? She had heard his speeches to his Society, heard him promise them a new order where they could rule over humans as they had been destined to do. But she could not believe it for a moment.

Whatever he was planning for the Stillworld, it was worse.

Hands clenched around the luminous, unyielding bars, Morgana raised a pale face toward the waxing moon.

"The moon," said Janie the next morning, "is rising later every day."

"You're telling me," said Charles. "We just barely beat Mom and Dad home last night. If they find us gone . . ."

Alys spoke heavily. "They'll be out till after midnight

tonight. They always are on Saturdays. That should give us enough time." She stared dully into a bowl of cereal. "I suppose."

No one answered. Four breakfasts sat uneaten on the table, and the comic page of the newspaper, which Charles generally read to Claudia in the morning, lay folded untouched on top of the homemaking section.

Seeing Cadal Forge face-to-face had changed everything.

"Hey—you could just *ask*," Charles said edgily as, without warning, Janie lunged across him to grab the paper.

"Where's the front page? Did Dad take it *again?*"

"Why?" said Alys.

"You wanted to know how much time we'll have tonight, didn't you? Well, the paper tells when the moon rises. And if it's rising late enough—after ten, say—"

"I know, Janie. Believe me, I'm already worrying."

"Worrying, as such," said Janie, "isn't going to do much good. I'm going to the little library to get an almanac and find out when moonrise is."

The little one-room library, located in the tiny Villa Park shopping center, was nestled against the City Hall. Janie wheeled her bike out of sight of the sheriff's cars, which were always parked in front of City Hall, and approached the library with averted face, nearly running into Danielle Selby at the door. Danielle was new at Janie's school, French on her mother's side, and a shoo-in for this year's cheerleading mascot. Janie muttered something in response to the other girl's friendly greeting and ducked around the librarian's counter to thumb through the pamphlet files. Most people weren't allowed behind the counter, but the librarians knew Janie well.

All Souls' Day, Alphabet, no *Almanac.* Janie opened a cupboard and stuck her head inside, looking for the scanty magazine files. Above her a voice called out.

"Hey, Dani—oh, there you are! I thought I saw you come in here. What're you doing?" The voice belonged to Bliss Bascomb, head cheerleader and by far the most beautiful girl at Cerro Villa Junior High.

"I have to renew this book," came Danielle's voice.

"Oh, homework, gah." Bliss made noises of appropriate disgust. "What's that for, English?"

"No—I was just reading it myself."

"Oh. Really?"

"It's a very interesting book."

A pause. Then: "Look, Dani, you aren't going to read again at lunch next week, are you? Like you did on Friday?"

"Why not? I got to practice on time."

"Oh, Dani." A heavy sigh. "Let me put it this way. I'm only saying this for your own good, right? You want to be mascot. Well, nobody's going to vote for a . . . for an— an *egghead.* I mean, you don't want to turn out like Janie Hodges-Bradley, do you? A walking encyclopedia?"

There was a choked sound from Danielle and noises indicative of frantic gesturing. Then a burst of hysterical laughter from Bliss and stifled wild giggling as both girls fled.

Behind the counter Janie knelt, staring sightlessly, her cheeks on fire.

"Why, hello, Janie," said the librarian. "I didn't see you down there. Are you finding what you need?"

Janie swallowed once, then stood without facing her.

"Thank you," she said expressionlessly. "I don't need anything at all."

When she got back the others were waiting.

"What took you so long?" said Alys. "Dad brought the paper home. It says the moon rises at nine-thirty-nine P.M. That should give us—hey! Where do you think you're going?"

The door of her bedroom locked behind her.

Presently Alys called softly, "Janie, we're going to the old house to have a conference. Don't you want to come?"

Silence.

"Janie, we have to go back *there* tonight. We're going to be very careful, but we have to go. Are you with us?"

Silence. Then Janie opened the door.

"I do not care how careful you are," she said, with precision. "Nor do I care what you do. I am similarly indifferent to the fate of Morgana, or for that matter to the fate of this entire stinking planet. Now leave me alone."

"Are you serious? You're not going with us?"

"Your perspicacity astonishes me."

"Cadal Forge will come through—"

"*Let him!*" Janie could not remember when she had screamed like that before. *"Just leave me alone!"* She slammed the door with all her strength in Alys's face.

All that day Janie stayed in her room, refusing even to come down for dinner. At eight o'clock, as she lay on her bed, she heard her parents leave, and at nine Alys knocked once again at the door. Janie ignored this and presently Alys and the others left, too.

The house was deadly quiet once they were gone. Heaving herself off the bed, Janie sat down at her desk with a book.

The words danced before her eyes, full of hidden meaning she could not extract. She read the beginning of the same sentence over and over, and each time before she reached the end she found herself staring over the top of the page into space. Not thinking, just staring.

She hoped something unspeakable happened to them in the Wildworld. She didn't know why she wanted this exactly, but it seemed to soothe the small volcano in her chest. She spent some minutes imagining just the sort of things that might happen to them. Then, after a glance at the desk clock, which showed it was after moonrise, she clenched her teeth so hard she felt a pain in her temples and returned to the book.

The effort of concentration was exhausting, especially on top of that bruised and aching feeling she'd had all day. Presently the chair began to feel very comfortable, and she thought she would just rest her eyes a moment before reading any more.

She woke with her head on the desk and a cramp in her shoulders, and sat up groggily, listening for the sound that had disturbed her sleep. A familiar sound . . . yes, the garage door opening. Now, why on earth should that send alarm signals tingling down all her nerve ends?

One look at the clock and she leapt out of the chair so quickly she bruised both knees on the desk. Ten after one! And she hadn't heard Alys and the others come home.

It was just possible they had come in without waking

her. But a moment later she had thrown open the door to Claudia's room and was looking at an empty bed.

Downstairs, a key turned in a lock. Her parents would not check up on Charles or Alys, but Claudia was another matter. One of them was bound to look in on her before going to bed.

Janie cast one wild glance around the room, then tore open the door to Claudia's closet. On the floor was a jumble of stuffed animals and toys, and one ancient battered doll which stood nearly three feet high. Its plastic face was smashed, and one blue eye rolled gruesomely loose in its head, but it had mouse-colored hair like Claudia's. Janie stuffed it under the covers of Claudia's bed, with its head on Claudia's pillow, and drew the blankets up all around. She just had time to hit the light switch and get into the hall before her parents appeared on the stairs.

"Hello," whispered her father. "Up so late?"

Conscious of her flushed cheeks and rapidly beating heart, she whispered back, "I thought I heard something, so I looked in Claudia's room to see if she was okay."

"Alys put her to bed on time?" Without waiting for an answer, her mother softly opened Claudia's door and peeped in. A moment later she softly closed it again. "Sleeping like an angel."

"She's a doll," agreed Janie involuntarily.

"Well, good-night. Don't go to sleep in your clothes."

"No. Good-night. 'Night, Dad."

Safely back in her own room, she collapsed on the bed and thumped the pillow with her fists. *Blast* Alys! Was she crazy, staying out so late? And keeping Claudia out, too. Didn't she realize the consequences?

And then, slowly, she raised her head from the tumbled bedclothes. Because of course Alys realized the consequences. She would never deliberately do this. Something was wrong.

Janie had never shinnied down a drainpipe before, and halfway down the one outside her window she fell, numbing her left arm and side. The night was cold and crystal clear, the half-moon sailing high in the sky as she rode to Morgana's. Shivering with anxiety and chill, she let herself in the back door to be greeted by echoing silence.

It was almost more than she could do to look through that dark, abandoned house. On the second floor she jumped, then darted into Morgana's bedchamber, only to find that what she had taken to be a knot of people was her own reflections in the double mirrors. Shaken, she pushed aside the tapestries around the bed and sat on it to think.

They were still in the Wildworld, all right. And what she was going to do about it she had no idea. What *could* she do? There was a rusty poker in the bedroom fireplace, and she picked it up and looked at it, then flung it back. Madness. If they had been captured by Cadal Forge's Society it would take an army to rescue them.

Anyway, it would serve them right. . . .

But the thought trickled away as she drew in her breath sharply, her eyes narrowing. Once again she reached for the poker and, weighing it thoughtfully in her hands, she turned to look speculatively at the mirrors.

"We have nothing to say to you." Alys's voice was hoarse, and she blinked away sweat that streamed into her eyes.

She was standing with Charles and Claudia, backed

against the wall, facing the sorcerei. There were five of them, tall and graceful, with inhuman smiles on their lips. Three had staffs.

Aric was one of these, and the Gray actually trembled in his hand as he contemplated the joy their capture would bring to Cadal Forge. His whole face was alight with happiness.

"You *will* speak to us, eventually, you know," he assured her, as he'd been assuring her for the past hour, and he held the Gray Staff to her throat, and smiled tenderly.

"Should we not fashion something to hold them?" asked one of the other sorcerei, and Aric was distracted.

"Yes," he said. "I'll cast a binding spell. Then my lord can deal with them at his leisure when he returns." He added something in a low voice which was lost on Alys.

Everything had gone amiss from the start that night, she thought helplessly. It had been all wrong not having Janie with them; it had thrown them off balance. Alys had decided that from now on they would hold their meetings in the barren nursery, the one mirrorless room in the old house. That way, even if the sorcerei had found a way to turn the mirrors into windows, they would be safe from spying.

They had determined to go through the mirror in the spinning-wheel room, the room next door to the nursery, and search the entire second floor. Cautiously, they had entered the Wildworld, and, cautiously, looked up and down the dark hallway before venturing out. To Alys's frustration and disappointment the rooms on either side of the spinning-wheel room were locked. But they had kept trying, creeping stealthily, like mice or shadows, through narrow corridors and candle-lit alcoves.

The silence and the tension had been difficult to bear, especially for Claudia, who was already tired. Charles had suggested, as they reached the far end of the wing, that they go home.

"It's enough for one trip," he whispered. "And, anyway, there's something here tonight, something I don't like. It *feels* wrong."

Alys, tired herself and unwilling to admit that she knew what Charles meant, had snapped out something cross, and turned the handle on the last door in the corridor.

And walked into a conclave of sorcerei.

The ensuing chase had brought them into the great hall, where the Gray Staff suddenly turned the air in front of them as solid as stone. The staff had done other things, too, since then, as Aric tried to persuade them to tell who had sent them and who their allies were. Fortunately, he hadn't tried very hard—yet, thought Alys, feeling her stomach muscles tighten. He would leave that to Cadal Forge.

Aric had begun the binding spell, scattering powder from a wallet at his belt while Gray, Azure, and Jade Green Staffs traced lines of colored fire in the air. Alys flinched. She had encountered those fire-lines trying to escape before, and they burned like acid. "Keep close," she whispered to Charles, hugging Claudia yet more tightly to her. "If something distracts them—just for a second . . ."

But nothing would, she knew. They could not hope for help. There was nothing in this world which was not hostile, and it was she, Alys, who had brought them here, she who was responsible.

That was the worst thing, the thing almost past endurance. Not the fear, although the Gray Staff had already made her more afraid than she had ever been in her life. Not the pain, or even the helplessness. But the knowledge that whatever happened to them now, it was her doing.

"Forgive me, Claudia," she whispered.

At that moment, on the stairway between the pillars, there was a movement like a prismatic waterfall.

"Janie?" For a moment Alys thought her beleaguered eyes were playing tricks on her. But it *was* Janies, it was a thousand Janies, an army of Janies flooding down the stairs. They were the size of a schoolgirl and the size of a pin and all sizes in-between and they flourished weapons that looked like pokers. Alys's legs gave way and her jaw sagged.

Endless Janies kept coming down the stairway, pokers raised. And then there were Janies beating Aric and Janies attacking the other sorcerei and Janies who thrashed at empty air. For every Janie that fell a dozen rose up in her place.

The abandoned fire-web shriveled to the ground and Charles and Claudia leapt free. Alys rose and tottered after them. The sorcerei, she realized, had not lost their heads. Even as they fought they placed themselves so as to guard each of the exits from the hall. But shrewd as they were, they had overlooked one thing.

"Get to a mirror!" shouted the Janies. Only it didn't sound that way. Some of them started shouting before others and some finished after, like a badly drilled chorus or a song sung in rounds. "G-g-g-get to a mirror-irror-irror-or-or," they shouted.

Protected by Janies on every side, Alys and the others forged their way toward the dais mirror. At the last second Alys turned to the nearest Janie, which was smaller than most and rainbow-colored around the edges. "But *you*—"

"Coming-coming-coming-coming!" Spurred on by the tidal wave of noise, Alys gained the dais and pitched forward.

In the human world, a cricket chirped.

"Where's Janie?" cried Charles, untangling himself from Claudia.

A voice rang out above them. One voice. "I'm in Morgana's bedroom"

They ran to meet her.

"How did you do that?" they chorused.

One Janie stood in the bedchamber, her hair tangled, a poker drooping from her hand. She staggered.

"You take on—the properties of the mirror you go through," she said raggedly. "Like the dark mirror," she added, seeing their blank faces. "El'mentary." She swayed and would have fallen if Charles had not caught her her.

"But—"

"Shadowy reflections make you shadows. So multiple reflections—" She gestured at the two full-length mirrors that faced one another in the alcove behind Morgana's bed, and in the mirrors endless Janies gestured with her.

"And now we'd better get home," she added tiredly. "before Mom and Dad find that doll in Claudia's bed."

Alys had been listening with a numb, befuddled expression. Now she started. "Before—oh, Janie, what time is it? What have you done?"

"It's late," said Janie, "and I'll explain on the way."

chapter 13

OUTSIDE IN THE
WILDWORLD

One more time," said Janie. "Bicycles in garage,
garage door unlocked. Pillows ready. Alarm clocks set—"

"And the foot bone's connected to the anklebone,"
said Charles. "Believe me, Janie, we've got it. Enough."

Afternoon sunlight slanted across the floor of the nursery where they sat, and a Sunday quiet pervaded the
outer world. But there was no peace here. The moon that
night would rise at 10:19 P.M., and they were going to
leave their beds secretly to go to the Wildworld.

The suggestion had been Janie's and Janie had dominated the discussion afterward. Alys was tense and with-
drawn, only nodding in silence when Janie said flatly that
they needed a new strategy. "They know about us now,"

Janie had pointed out. "There aren't enough of them to guard *all* the mirrors, but we can't just wander around the castle anymore."

"What else *can* we do?" said Charles.

Janie had told them. Her idea was that they should forget about looking for Morgana and should concentrate instead on getting a message to the Weerul Council. The Council might not be entirely trustworthy, but it had a history of wanting to keep Wildfolk in the Wildworld, and it was far better equipped to deal with Cadal Forge than they. And the Council was the only thing the Society seemed to be afraid of.

The idea was so logical that Charles said he was surprised they hadn't thought of it before.

"Why didn't the vixen tell us to do that?" said Claudia.

Janie glanced at the silent Alys, then lowered her spiky lashes. "Well . . . she was probably thinking of Morgana." She raised her purple eyes to look around at them all. "I mean, Morgana's back in the Wildworld—you see? She's breaking the law as much as Cadal Forge is. And I believe the vixen said the penalty was death."

"Then we *can't*," said Claudia, and Charles almost simultaneously added, "We promised the vixen—"

"There are only five more days till the solstice," said Janie, and watched Charles slowly shut his open mouth, his protests dying unvoiced.

Claudia saw this, too, and in dismay she turned to Alys with pleading blue eyes. "Alys—"

"Oh, I don't *know*," said Alys. "I don't like it, but nothing I've done or thought so far has been right. Janie, how *could* we get a message to them?"

"I don't know any way. But . . . the serpent might."

Alys threw up her hands. "Do what you want, then. Claudia, I'm sorry."

Tears welled in Claudia's eyes, and she fell silent.

And so it was decided. They would each take an alarm clock to bed that night, set for eleven-thirty. By that time their parents would be asleep. When the alarms went off they would stuff pillows under their bedclothes, dress, and climb out their respective windows. The pillows would fool any parent who happened to look in, and as long as they were back in their beds by morning no one would ever know.

Everything went just as planned. At ten minutes to midnight they were all gathered in the garage, Claudia heavy-eyed and stumbling, the older three prickling with alertness. Silently they wheeled their bicycles into the night, where a three-quarter moon hung low in the sky.

The cold air woke Claudia but she remained listless, and Alys was terribly subdued as they approached the conservatory mirror. Charles volunteered, tersely, to go first and scout around and Alys simply shrugged. He reappeared a moment later with the news that the conservatory was unguarded, and they all followed.

The tangle of riotous greenery was the same as they had left it, a small jungle in the moonlight. Only, now, menace seemed to lurk everywhere as they crept through the vines and underbrush to the shining grotto full of treasure. Alys called for the serpent in a voice no louder than the slow, lonely dripping of water from a stalactite into one of the grotto pools.

There was a whisper of movement and the serpent's

blue and coral body, a jewel itself, flowed up a pile of gold. Alys knelt and stretched out her hands.

"We need your help," she said.

"If I had my wings—" said the serpent, some time later. It broke off, trembling with frustration.

"Don't blame yourself," said Alys dully. "There's no chance, then, of getting word to the Council?"

"Of all the Finderlais—all the Wildfolk—only serpents and Quislais have the power to travel fast enough. And the sorcerei, with their portals. If I had my wings—"

"There couldn't be another serpent nearby?"

The serpent hissed and swayed. "There are no other great houses to be guarded here. Fell Andred—" It stopped. "Might I be so bold as to curl my tail about your wrist, Lady Alys? I thank you. That comforts me. Fell Andred is isolated because the Chaotic Zone to the north is so near. Each time the Well of Chaos erupts, the destruction comes closer. To the east are the marshes and on the west and south is Elwyn's Wood. Only elementals live in the marshes—and even stranger creatures which some say crawl there from the Chaotic Zone. And in the Wood . . ." A shudder undulated down its body.

"Did you say *Elwyn's* Wood?"

"Elwyn Silverhair runs wild there sometimes with the Dirdreth, the wood elementals. But I beg you, my lady, not to go near the place. You would be in peril of your life. The Dirdreth answer to no law but Elwyn's and they have little love for strangers."

"We have no reason for going there," said Alys, cradling her head in her free hand. "It sounds as if—what, Charles?"

"I heard something," said Charles tensely. "There—again. Like somebody moving . . . Alys, we'd better go—"

"My lady! Quickly—"

There was a nightmarish moment as they scrambled off their knees and then an instant in which time froze as Alys saw the faces of sorcerei clearly framed in the tangle of black bushes. The sorcerei were between them and the mirror.

"Quickly, quickly! To the back of the grotto! There is a way out—"

Alys never knew if she was responding to the serpent's voice or to blind panic, but she grabbed a fistful of Claudia's jacket and shoved her forward and ran. The grotto narrowed toward the back, became a slippery tunnel with jagged, bruising floor and walls. Behind them were the sounds of pursuit. The only light came from luminous jewels about them, but they thrashed and skidded desperately on, as the narrow hole turned downward and twisted on itself. Stones cut at them and tore their clothing. Confused shouting filled their ears. They ran and fell and ran again. And then the floor simply disappeared beneath them and they were sliding and tumbling, out of control, for what seemed an eternity, until they burst out into the moonlight, on the hill below the castle.

Charles picked himself up at once, and gave one hand each to Janie and Claudia. "Don't stop! Keep on going!"

He was off like a deer. They fled down the hill, Fell Andred's square stone bulk looming behind them. The moonlight made it almost bright as day, but colors were strange and distances deceptive.

Once Alys looked over her shoulder, and seemed to see

lights moving on the hill. It was hard to tell, for a mist was rising about them, blowing in from the east, but they looked like torches. With a sob, she set her face forward and ran on. They were all exhausted now, legs trembling, breath wheezing, the blood pounding in their ears. They fell again and again as the mist rose thicker, casting a white veil all around them. Dimly, Alys felt that something was wrong, but the thought was confused with the pounding in her head. It was not until the mist had become a white wall, as thick and opaque as the air between the mirrors, that she realized the serpent was calling her.

It had wound its way up her arm and coiled around her neck to cry directly into her ear. Even so, its thin, reedy voice was barely audible. "My lady! Lady Alys! Please stop!"

She was utterly alone, there was nothing to see anywhere but fog. "Claudia!" she screamed, her voice deadened and muffled. Claudia stumbled out of the mist and collapsed at her feet, trying not to cry.

"Janie!" Limping, her face white as the mist, Janie appeared. Without a word she sat down.

"Charles!"

In the long silence that followed Alys felt herself turn slowly toward her sisters. Claudia had frozen in the middle of wiping her cheeks, and Janie had lifted her drooping head, listening.

"Charles? Charles! Charles!"

They were all looking at her now, Alys realized. Even the serpent. They all expected her to have some answer to this. Panic rose in her, and with it the need to *do*. "Stay here," she gasped to Janie. "Both of you, just stay here. I'll find him and come back. I'll—" Without finishing the sentence she plunged into the mist, shouting, "Stay there!"

For a long time she ran in confusion, the mist burning in her lungs, shouting Charles's name. The serpent was limp around her neck. When she could no longer run she staggered, and when she could no longer shout she croaked. What brought her up short at last was that the ground, which had been growing damper and more unreliable with every step, now gave out entirely, and she found herself up to her ankles in water.

"The Eldreth marshes, lady," whispered the exhausted serpent.

"The marshes . . ." Mud sucked at her shoes, releasing them with a reluctant squelch. Hoarsely, she called for Charles, but each step she took seemed to land her in deeper water. She would have to go back. . . .

It was only then she realized that she did not know where "back" was.

"What am I going to do?" She spoke quite softly, in despair, as the full impact of her situation hit her. The serpent looked at her with gentle surprise.

"The marshes are dangerous, it is true, but for a great hero such as yourself . . ."

Alys bit her lips to keep from screaming. "I'm not a great hero," she said. "Please don't say that."

"O my lady." The serpent's faint voice was reproachful. "It is you who must not say that. You who, in your wisdom, are worthy to sit in majesty with the Council. You—"

"I am *not,*" cried Alys, pulling the serpent away from her neck. The frustration of the last days overwhelmed her and poured out in a rush. "Don't you understand? I've done everything wrong, everything, right from the start. Every decision I've made has been a disaster! I lied to the police, I let Cadal Forge see me, I let us get caught by Aric. What they could have done to us, to Claudia . . . And now Charles is lost, and *I'm* lost, and I'm *scared*. And I don't want anyone relying on me anymore. I can't stand it!"

Roughly thrusting the serpent back onto her jacket, she splashed violently off in what she hoped was the direction she had come from. There was nothing to guide her but the feel of the land itself: As soon as she got to dryer ground she tried to stay on it. Each time a foot sank in mud she yanked and pulled, and when the muck at last let it free with a *pop*, she went on in another direction.

The serpent was very still inside her jacket. She wished she hadn't spoken so harshly to it. She hoped it wouldn't talk anymore because if it did she was going to say something worse. Her foot sank again, and she threw her weight back, trying to lift it. Lord, this mud was deep! It sucked at her as if it were a living thing that wouldn't let go. There, her foot was coming up.

This time there was no *pop* of release, only a long squelch, and as she pulled her foot slowly up she saw, to her horror, that attached to her ankle were a mud-colored hand and arm. The arm came from somewhere down below, and as she stared at it in disbelief, suddenly it yanked harder and her whole leg shot into the hole. Now she could scream. She clawed desperately at the earth, but it crumbled wetly away and she felt herself being pulled down. Whole tussocks of grass came with her and then the sides of the hole crashed in and she plummeted, screaming, into the ground.

The thing had let go of her foot as she fell, and now by the opalescent light of moon and mist above, she could see it. It was shaped vaguely like a very tall man, and its long gray arms and legs were covered with matted hair and mud. A terrible stench arose from it. Its feet were clawed like a bird's, but the knobby fingers which had locked with such strength on her ankle ended in long twisted nails. Then the moonlight shone on its face, and she screamed again, for it *had* no face, only an open, gaping wound of a mouth, with pendulous wattles of skin hanging below.

Eyeless, earless, it scrabbled along the ground with its hands, searching for her. She was too frightened to reach for her dagger, too frightened even to scream any more. Her mind and body paralyzed, she lay among the splintered bones on the floor of the den, waiting for death. And then *it* screamed, a high unearthly shriek, and turning her eyes to the ground, she saw something like a blue and coral necklace. The serpent struck at the birdlike feet again and again, and the feet clawed back wildly. Alys felt the cold hilt of the gannelin dagger beneath her fingers, but she could not summon up the will to move. Then, with a vicious swipe, the talons sent the serpent flying, its small body cracking like a whip before it struck the wall.

"No, oh, no," sobbed Alys. She wanted, not to run, but to curl in a ball and die. The hands with their twisted nails were searching for her again, and she whimpered and shrank back from them. As one found her, and closed on her arm, she struck feebly at it with the gannelin knife, and blood sprayed across her face. The shrieking grew unbearable then, as she slashed at the creature's fleshless arms and legs, but in the chaos of noise and blood she realized that she was only infuriating it, and that all the while it was drawing her nearer with an irresistible strength.

For one clear moment she saw it reared high above her, its mouth wide open with shrieking—and in her mind's eye she saw the serpent, limp and perhaps lifeless on the floor.

Thrown or wielded it will not easily miss its mark. . . .

Wrenching her right arm free she changed her grip on the dagger, and with all her strength threw it straight at the gaping mouth. The shrieking broke off as if the dagger had severed it. For a moment the creature tottered, and Alys fell backward as it released her to claw at its own face with its nails. And then, with a shudder, the whole stringy, stinking bulk of it crashed down beside her.

The dagger, jarred loose by the impact, plopped down. Alys lay without touching it for a long time, and cried.

Her body was bruised all over, and there were bloody furrows on her arms where the crooked nails had gouged her. When she rose at last, her legs would barely support her. Still crying and shuddering, she searched with her hands in the nameless muck at the bottom of the lair until she found the serpent. She looped its flaccid body about her wrist and crawled back to the dagger. It was stained a deep muddy red and she could hardly bring herself to touch it. Somehow, sobbing, she clambered out of the pit and began to stagger through the marsh.

The mist had thinned, and the moon shone down on her, but she was too dazed to tell where she was going. She only knew that she must not stop, and that there was danger everywhere. Clutching the serpent to her, stiffly pointing the dagger straight ahead, she stumbled on. Her legs were heavy and aching. She made them keep moving. A muddy red fog swam in her brain. Then the dagger seemed to go double before her eyes as a great wave of dizziness overtook her and the red fog turned to black.

chapter 14

MARSH AND WOOD

$Alys$ was dreaming of eyes. Green-brown eyes, the color of the marsh, so large they made the small brown face they were set in seem even smaller by comparison. They looked down on her with an expression both keen and compassionate, and they wanted her to sleep . . . to sleep. . . .

She woke to a gentle rocking motion.

"What—where—?" She started up, heedless of the pain in her head, her voice a whispery croak—and met the eyes from her dream.

"Hush," said the creature belonging to the eyes, pressing her back gently. But Alys had seen enough. She was in a boat, a small, flat boat piloted by two more of the sleek brown creatures, and the marsh was slipping away beneath her.

"I am Arien Edgewater of the Eldreth—the marsh dwellers," said the lissome little creature, and Alys blinked stupidly at her in wonder. The elemental's supple body was much longer than her slender arms and legs, and she had small, clever-looking hands, with fur on the backs but not on the soft palms. The same velvety fur covered her body and framed her face as if she were wearing a hood, and her only garment was a sort of open, sleeveless coat, made of gossamer material. The other two marsh elementals wore nothing.

"Where—" began Alys again. Her throat was raw.

A soft hand stroked her forehead. "We are traveling to the edge of the marsh, to a place of healing. It is not much farther. Rest."

Alys shook her head. "No. Please. Where—is serpent?"

"Ah." The green-brown eyes turned grave, and were covered for an instant by eyelids which slid sideways over them. Then a basket was placed gently beside Alys, a small basket of woven reeds. In the bottom, on a bed of leaves, the serpent was coiled, motionless. Its eyes were no longer like shining black glass beads, but milky and opaque, fixed.

"Is it—dead?"

"No. And I think it will not die if we reach the healing pool soon enough. Feathered guardians are strong. When my people found you lying senseless in the water I feared for you both. But, with luck, all will be well."

Alys lay still for a minute, looking up at the moon. Then, painfully, feeling the boat rock beneath her, she propped herself on one elbow and sat up again. The mist was still there, hanging low and ragged over the surface of the water. But the marsh itself had changed since she had first stumbled into it.

Strange and fantastic trees took shape out of the mist and were cloaked again as the boat passed, and bizarre vegetation rippled on the surface of the water. Yet, for all its lushness, this world was absolutely silent.

"It is the influence of the Chaotic Zone," said Arien Edgewater when Alys looked at her questioningly. "Wild magic has leaked out and changed this place. As it changes everything." And as Alys leaned against the side of the boat and listened, too tired and befuddled to think or speak, the marsh dweller told her about Chaotic Zones. How they blossomed suddenly when the deep core magic found its way to the surface of the Wildworld, bursting through faults to form Wells of Chaos. How the Chaos spread in all directions from a Well, forming a Chaotic Zone, and how it receded every so often only to flood forth again. She told Alys about the destruction left behind when a Chaotic Zone did recede. Sometimes, to be sure, the Chaos left something strange and beautiful, like the perpetual glacier the Selessor had set in the midst of a desert, or the burning meadows of Balinarch. But usually it was simply desolation, charred and barren wasteland in which no life stirred except the twisted life the Chaos itself created.

"Like the lurking thing you killed," said Arien, and Alys looked away, the pain and confusion in her mind worse than the aching of her body.

"I was afraid," she said. "And I waited too long to strike at it—and you haven't even asked me who I am," she finished suddenly, almost accusingly, turning back.

The green-brown eyes were serene. "You have been

hurt," said Arien Edgewater, "and you travel with a Feathered Serpent, and you have killed a very evil thing which has menaced my people long. That is all I need to know. But perhaps," she added softly, "there is more you need to tell."

Alys felt a surge of anger, and then she realized that she did want to tell this marsh woman more. She needed to. Trembling with agitation, she let the whole story pour out of her: her promise to the vixen, her attempts to keep it, and her failures. All her failures. Defiantly, one by one, she set them before Arien Edgewater. The letter, Cadal Forge, Aric.

And the mud monster. Tonight, because of her, the serpent had almost been killed.

"And now look at what I've come to," she ended, holding out her hands with a short, bitter laugh. "Covered with mud, and Charles and the others all lost somewhere in the mist. Who'd've believed it of good old responsible Alys? Good old practical, punctual, sensible, responsible Alys!"

There was a pause while Arien Edgewater gazed out at the marsh. When the elemental spoke, without turning, it was very gravely. "You are responsible," she replied, ignoring everything else Alys had said. "You are responsible for what will happen to you next, you are the creator of your own future. And you are what you are . . . because you have chosen to be."

"But I *didn't* choose! Or, if I did, I'm changing my mind now. I just can't take the responsibility any longer. I just can't take it!"

"Where, then, will you leave it?" said Arien Edgewater.

Before Alys could gather her wits to form a reply, the rowers paused and the marsh woman added, in an entirely different tone, "Here you can see the wake of a Chaotic Zone."

Gray in the moonlight, a desert of mud stretched out from the marsh. Nothing rose above that mud, not a twig or branch or leaf. Alys couldn't see the end of it.

It smelled like the lurking creature's lair. Alys shuddered, and then she realized that Arien Edgewater was getting out of the boat. "You're not going into *that*?"

One of the rowers handed Arien the serpent's basket. "I must," she said. "The pool I spoke of is there."

"In a Chaotic Zone?"

"In the very Well itself. When the Chaos recedes the pool is left. Wait here, and I will return with the water of it." Carrying the basket, the slender elemental set out across the mud flats.

"She is the only one who goes into that place," said a rower softly as they watched. "And even she does not go often, only when there is much need."

"You mean," said Alys, "that *nobody* else has ever been there? No one but her?"

"Three times since she found the pool the Chaos has welled up and flooded to the very edge here. The danger is always great. No one else dares go."

Alys hung on to the side of the boat, head lowered, eyes shut. She knew what she ought to do. But she was wounded, she was tired, she had every excuse in the world for not doing it. Arien herself had told her to stay. No one would ever know, or blame her.

Awkwardly, almost capsizing the boat, she tumbled out and floundered in the water toward the mud of the Zone.

"Come back! There is no need for *you* to go!" cried one of the rowers excitedly, and the other added mysteriously, "You have not been *invited!*"

Alys's answer was a shake of her head as she slogged through the mud in the trail of Arien's footprints. She could not explain it even to herself, but for the first time since Aric had held the Gray Staff to her throat her course was clear.

Arien Edgewater slowed as Alys reached her, and after one long searching look, she gave Alys the basket.

"Come, then," she said.

All the way they walked the ground was the same: dark gray mud, sticky as tar, smelling of decay. Alys was ready to jump at shadows, but nothing moved except them.

The marsh and the boat were long out of sight by the time they came to the pool. It was surrounded by flat gray rocks and surprisingly small. A bare inch or two of water lay on top of the gray silt that formed its bottom.

"The water seeps up very slowly, year after year," said Arien Edgewater. "We try to be sparing."

Alys knelt beside her. As she did, a wonderfully sweet smell wafted up to her, a clean, delicious smell that put the stench of the mud right out of her mind. She looked at the pool with new eyes, and saw that the water, though shallow, was clear as crystal. And clinging to the gray rock, with its roots in the water, was a little, low plant. When Alys gently stirred its dark green leaves with one finger she found hidden under them a flower, white in the moonlight, veined with silver. The blossom was no larger than her thumbnail.

All this time the fragrance of the pool drifted up to her, and when Arien Edgewater invited her with a gesture to bathe her face in it she obeyed eagerly. The water was icy cold and wherever it touched it left her feeling clean and strong, refreshed. The wounds on her arms closed as a few drops fell on them. When she had finished, Arien gently took the limp serpent and coiled it in the water, which just covered it.

"I will come back every day and tend to it until it is healed," she said, and Alys knew she would come, in spite of the danger, never touching the water herself.

"Why?" she said.

Arien Edgewater smiled. "Why did you come to the Wildworld?"

Alys looked down. "Someone had to," she said slowly, "and . . ."

"And?"

"And . . . there wasn't anyone else." Alys shut her eyes and took a deep breath of the pool's fragrance. When she opened her eyes again it was as if she were seeing Arien for the first time. "I have been very stupid," she said, "thinking I could give up because I've been making mistakes. Making mistakes doesn't mean you're a failure, does it? It only means you're trying. And there are some things you just can't turn back on."

"You *can* . . ."

"You can, but that won't make them go away. And you've got to turn around again sometime." Alys sat back. "I know all this *now*," she said. "When I leave will I forget?"

Very carefully, the elemental reached down into the little plant and snapped off the flower. Its scent was the scent of the pool. She laid it in Alys's hand.

"Keep this and remember," she said. "It is called malthrum, and it will never fade. And now," she added, "come back with me to my home, and rest."

Alys touched a petal of the tiny flower with one finger. Then her hand closed around it and she looked up, steadily.

"I'm sorry," she said, rising. "But I can't. I'd be grateful if you'd take me back to the edge of the marsh, though. You see, my brother and sisters are lost, and I have to find them."

Charles had run until he ran into a tree.

For some time he'd been tripping over roots and underbrush, and now, as he disentangled himself from the low, twisted branches, there was no mistake. He was in Elwyn's Wood. The shock of this realization, and the simple act of stopping, helped restore his senses. They shouldn't run anymore, they should sit down and figure out what to do next. He was surprised that Alys hadn't thought of that. In fact, where was . . .

The second shock was much worse than the first.

They had all been running together, falling together, picking each other up. But as the effort of running became torture he had focused only on himself. Now, he couldn't remember the last time he'd heard one of the others.

After a moment he shouted, "Alys?"

The silence that followed told him everything.

After another moment he began to walk.

He walked between trees to other trees. At their roots grew phantom orchids and bindweed, enchanter's nightshade and fairybells, and tiny ruffled mushrooms which glowed like foxfire. Nowhere was there any sign of a clearing.

Don't panic, he told himself. Don't panic; *whistle*.

He whistled his way along for almost two minutes before something whistled back.

Bird? Maybe. He stopped whistling in case it was the kind of bird that was attracted by music. Thereafter the silence was broken only by the crunching of dead leaves under his feet, and by the little shuffling noises behind him—or were they to the left of him? He began to walk faster. Now the noises were to the right. *And* to the left. And—

He almost walked into the girl.

Her pale face shone out of the mist. She had a sweet, wild smile, and the moonlight reflected from her eyes.

Rustling noises behind him. Charles turned hastily to see another girl there. This one had a hunting horn slung over her shoulder.

More of the smiling, dark-clad girls appeared. Looking into their slanted silvery eyes Charles was overcome by the sudden absolute conviction that he was seeing the Dirdreth.

"Um . . ." He gulped and tried to smile. "Excuse me. Excuse me—please—but I have to . . ."

The two nearest linked hands to bar his way. Instead of answering him they spoke to each other.

"What shall we do with him, crimson and saffron? Pluck him and make him a cushion to sit on?"

There was ringing laughter. Charles looked down at his yellow windbreaker and red shirt nervously. They were all holding hands, now, in an undulating ring around him.

Charles turned round and round in his tracks, trying to confront each speaker in turn.

"Put him in earth, then, or put him in water."

"Put him in limestone and teach him to wander!"

"Come, he's a pretty one—"

"Deela says keep him!"

"Give him a draught and don't trouble his sleeping!"

The circle began to revolve the other way.

"What shall we do with him, poor little mankin?"

A dozen voices rose in answer: "Take him to Elwyn! Take him to Elwyn!"

Laughing, singing, they surged around him, forcing him to walk, and then run, in the direction of their choice.

"But I don't *want* to—"

They took no notice of his protests. If he stumbled or slowed many hands bore him up. The girls ran like greyhounds, as lightly and effortlessly as the wind. Charles had lost track of time when at last the hunting horn sounded and was echoed from in front of them, and the wild girls slowed. They parted ranks before him and he stumbled into a clearing.

Heavy, night-blooming flowers hung from the trees on all sides. There were dozens of elementals, watchful, half-hidden by the veils of mist. And in the center of the circle, between mist and moonlight, sat Elwyn Silverhair.

"Do please sit down," she said, and smiled at him.

Charles felt fear give way to anger.

"I don't want to sit down!" he snapped. "I didn't ask to come here at all, and you have no call to keep me. I—I demand my rights!"

Elwyn leaned her head on one side, puzzled. Of all the creatures he had seen in the Wildworld, she was the loveliest—and the strangest. The human world could never have produced such perfect delicacy of feature, such liquid grace of movement. A faint, insubstantial light hung about her, haloing her every gesture.

"You don't want to sit down?" she said.

"All I want is to get out of these stinking woods!"

Laughter from the wood elementals.

Elwyn Silverhair looked more puzzled than ever. "But you came into these stinking woods of your own will," she pointed out reasonably. "You might as well enjoy them." With her own hands she took a jeweled cup and, dipping up water from a flowing spring beside her, offered it to him.

Charles, thirsty after all the running, hesitated. But as he reached for the cup, several things flashed through his mind at once, forming a collage rather than a series of impressions. The vixen saying, "Luring young men into the Wildworld and then dumping them back twenty years later." The serpent: "You would be in peril of your life." The legends of Rip Van Winkle and Tam Lin. And the wild, merry voices of the wood spirits: "Give him a draught and don't trouble his sleeping!"

His hand fell back. "No thanks."

Elwyn laughed and tilted the cup to her own lips. The eyes which looked at him over the rim were as blue as cornflowers, the same color as the jewels in the wide belt over her kirtle. She wore a small cap covered with pearls and sapphires, and beneath it the diaphanous veil of her hair was like moonlight.

"Well, now!" she said when she lowered the cup. "Who are you, boy, and what do you want in Elwyn's Wood?"

"I'm Charles, and I—listen, I'll tell you what I'm doing here! I'm here because of *you!*"

"Yes?" she said. Her lashes were as silver as her hair.

"Because of what you—*listen.* Do you know where Morgana is now?"

Elwyn thought. "No. I saw her some time ago, but . . . Do you like music? I do." She nodded to a wild girl, who began to play a flute, all in a minor key.

"Do you realize what Cadal Forge is *planning?*"

Elwyn pursed her bright lips. "Cadal Forge spoke rudely to me once," she mused.

Charles stared. "Did he? Did he really?"

"Perhaps I just dreamed it. Do you dream?"

"Have you understood a single thing I've said?"

"Of course I've understood a single thing you've said. You're a Charles and you're not thirsty. But perhaps you'd care for something to eat?"

Charles sat down and put his head in his hands. He was stranded in an alien world with a mentally incompetent midget—

"How old are you, anyway?" he mumbled.

"Old? Oh, I'm *old.* I've no idea, really. Why, do you think it matters?"

—with a mentally incompetent midget who didn't even know her own age. And no way of leaving. And who knew what might be happening to Alys and the others.

"You're not ill, are you? If you like I can try to figure it out."

Charles raised his head listlessly. "Figure what out?"

"How old I am. It may take me awhile. . . ."

Charles sat up straight. Elwyn Silverhair was looking at

him anxiously, hands clasped under her chin. The worst thing was that he was beginning to like her. Sure, she was out to lunch as far as reality was concerned, but there was no malice in her and she was prettier than Bliss Bascomb.

"That's all right," he said. Faintly ashamed of his bad temper, he leaned over to scoop some water out of the spring.

"Don't," said Elwyn quickly, as he bent his head to drink. "Unless you *want* to be a fish, of course."

The water trickled through his fingers as he stared at her.

The mist was thinning, and at the edge of the circle Charles spotted a newcomer to Elwyn's group, a young boy wearing breeches like Elwyn's maidens, but no shirt. He looked slightly less wild than the girls. As Elwyn spread a cloth and put out bread and cheese, Charles casually edged over to the youth and spoke out of the side of his mouth.

"Hey, look, do you happen to know the way out of these woods?" he murmured. " 'Cause, you know, this place is pretty weird, and I've gotta go."

The silence that followed was so long that at last Charles turned to look at his companion. For a moment longer the boy gazed at him out of cinnamon-colored eyes without speaking. Then, with no warning at all, he threw back his head and howled like a wolf.

In three long bounds Charles was back in the circle beside Elwyn.

"Honey, or butter?" said she.

He sat down and put his head in his hands.

"Look," he said, some minutes later. "I'm going to try

to explain. There were some people with me, and we got separated. Maybe your friends here saw them?"

"Deela?" said Elwyn.

A copper-haired girl stepped forward. "Some time ago we saw three others. They were small but clumsy, mistress. Not unlike *him*, but less brightly colored."

"Right," said Charles grimly, and rounded on Elwyn. "Those small clumsy things were my sisters. And now I'm lost, and they're lost, and we're not even lost together. And the whole reason we're in this world at all is you. So"—belligerently—"what are you going to do about it?"

Elwyn offered him a piece of bread, saw by his expression that this was not sufficient, and tried again. "We could sing and dance in the moonlight," she suggested.

"No," said Charles.

"We could listen to sweet music and count stars. . . ."

"No."

She bit her lip, wrung her hands, and made a tremendous effort. "I—I could send Deela to fetch your sisters here?"

"*Please*," said Charles. "Please do that and then show all of us the way out of these woods."

And so, with long shivering cries and bursts of melodious laughter, Deela and several of the other elementals departed. Charles flung himself to the ground and concentrated on not looking at his watch.

Time crawled by, and presently even strange flute music seemed lulling. He fell asleep.

He was awakened by a hunting horn, and as he sat up Deela loped smoothly into the circle. Behind her the wild girls herded a single weary figure.

"Alys!" cried Charles. *"What did you do with the others?"* he said to the girls.

Alys was pale, but quite calm and resolute. Squatting on her heels in the center of the clearing, she even managed to make herself understood by Elwyn.

"We're going to have to think of some way to scout around," she said. "I came with the wild girls because I suspected that they might have taken Charles, but I was hoping it wasn't just him. Because, you see, I've just been with the Eldreth, and they say Janie and Claudia aren't on the marsh. And now the Dirdreth tell me they aren't anywhere in the Wood. So the question is—where in the Wildworld are they?"

chapter 15

CASTLE

Janie and Claudia had watched Alys plunge into the mist. It had closed behind her before Janie got up the breath to shout.

"Wait a minute! You're coming back to find us—*how?* Alys!" As her cries were met by silence Janie turned around. "Oh, this is just terrific," she muttered, striking her palm rhythmically with a clenched fist. "This just absolutely *takes the cake*. What's wrong with her anyway?" she added with a change in tone. "Alys should know better."

"I think," sniffled Claudia from her forlorn seat on the ground, "that Aric scared her. She said when he got us that she wasn't—wasn't compliment to make decisions anymore."

"Com-pe-tent," said Janie. There was a terrible sinking

feeling inside her. But why? She had always resented her older sister's take-charge manner; Janie didn't enjoy being bossed. Only now . . .

If Alys goes down, she thought with sudden conviction, we are all lost.

Claudia sniffled again, and Janie looked at her with new eyes. She had never had much to do with Claudia before this sorcery business started, and Claudia, for her part, always went running to Alys or Charles when she had a problem. Now Charles had disappeared and Alys had gone amok and there was no one left but Janie.

"All right," she said, sitting down near Claudia and trying to sound cheerful—or at least competent. "We'll wait here awhile. You lie down and rest."

Obediently, Claudia curled on her side and pretended to sleep. Janie, looking at her pinched, quivering lips and her screwed-up eyelids, would have laughed if she hadn't felt so much like crying. Suddenly she wished very much that she had been the kind of sister Claudia would come running to.

"Janie?"

"Hmmm?" She lifted her chin off her drawn-up knees.

"Could—could we hold hands?"

Janie's mouth opened, and then she silently took Claudia's square, cold little hand in hers. Just for the moment she could think of nothing to say.

They were both chilled through by the time the mist cleared enough for them to see the stars. This was what Janie had been waiting for, and she tugged at the drowsing Claudia's hand.

"Come on," she said. "We're going to the castle. It's

the one place we all know, and if the others have any sense they'll head for it, too."

"But how?" Claudia rubbed her eyes. "How can we—"

"We go west. You know how to find west?"

Claudia looked at her hands. One was right and the other was left, and west had something to do with it. . . .

"Never mind. I'll show you how to find the North Star as we walk. After that, west is easy."

It took a long time, walking back, but as they got farther from the marsh the mist disappeared and they saw the moonlight shining on the high hill of Fell Andred. The moon was sinking before them as they climbed the hill.

"Keep very quiet," whispered Janie, helping Claudia over the ruins of the outer courtyard wall. "*They'll* still be looking for us." The castle, which offered their only safety, was also their greatest danger.

"I'm thirsty," Claudia whispered back.

Janie thought. They were as likely to fall into the castle well as to get water out of it. But she had seen a fountain in the gardens behind the conservatory.

Noiselessly, they made their way through the tangled greenery (for the gardens also had run wild) to the fountain. Though the stone basin was cracked and green with age, a trickle of water still seeped through the moss at the top.

"Now I'm hungry," whispered Claudia, when they had both had a cool, slightly scummy drink.

"The kitchen garden," said Janie curtly, "is on the other side of the castle. But maybe there's something here."

Claudia looked doubtful. But they were hungry enough to try foraging on the weed-choked, chilly winter ground. And in their hunger and frustration they forgot to watch the castle.

Which explains why it was such a terrible shock when Janie looked up and saw the sorcerer.

It was Aric, and he had his staff. Recognition, anger, and a hideous sort of joy chased one another across his face. He started toward them.

"Run!" screamed Janie. But Claudia stood paralyzed like a rabbit transfixed by a headlight.

Janie had no poker now. Everything inside her wanted to run and keep running. Then her hands balled into fists and her teeth clenched and she *was* running, but running toward Aric instead of away from him. There was a rock in her path. It felt good in her hand, rough and solid. As Aric reached Claudia, Janie drew back her arm the way Alys had taught her, and threw, and the rock hit Aric in the stomach.

The sorcerer did not even break stride, but he forgot about Claudia and veered. He remembered Janie. His lips drew back from his teeth. In the heat of his anger he raised his staff as if to club her down rather than ensorcel her.

Suddenly a bolt of silver light hit him from behind, forming a nimbus about him and shimmering hazily in the air as he pitched forward onto his face.

Janie goggled.

Near the ruined grotto wall stood a woman holding a staff which glinted frostily in the moonlight. When Aric did not move, she lowered it and walked unhurriedly up to them.

"You do not look particularly dangerous," she commented, studying them each in turn. "What have you done to earn the wrath of this foolish man?"

"I—we—" This woman was Somebody, you could tell that at a glance. She was as tall as Cadal Forge, with an air that was at once imperial and gracious. Her gown was midnight blue worked with silver, and her braided hair, bound with a silver circlet, was dark red. Rings set with blue and white gems glinted on her fingers.

"Come, do I look so fearsome as all that?" The woman smiled as she raised the cowering Claudia. "If you are hungry you shall be fed," she added, with a penetrating glance at the tuber that hung from Claudia's hand.

Janie hesitated.

"Are you—a sorceress?"

The woman inclined her head.

"Are you—are you with Cadal Forge?"

The woman's expression changed; her cheeks darkened with blood, and she seemed about to make an angry retort. Then, with a visible effort, she composed herself.

"Do not utter that name in my presence again," she said, very quietly. "No, I will not hurt you—you are children and know nothing of what he has done. But do not speak his name."

"But we *do* know what he's done," said Claudia eagerly, forgetting to be frightened. "That's why we're here."

A puzzled frown creased the woman's brow.

"I can explain," said Janie, coming to a sudden decision. "But to do that I'll have to mention C—I mean, that name you told us not to utter. Him." She jerked a thumb at the castle.

"This interests me mightily," breathed the woman, looking at Janie with narrowed eyes. "Come, let us sit here by the fountain. You have my leave to speak."

"But what about Aric? Will he wake up?"

"In three days' time." With a courtly gesture the woman ushered them to the fountain, out of sight of the house, and they sat down.

"It's like this," said Janie, and, carefully and precisely, she told of how the vixen had summoned them and how they had made the amulet and tried to find Morgana. She told of Cadal Forge's Society, and his plans for the Stillworld.

The woman's reaction was unexpected. As the story went on she began to smile as if amused, and when Janie finished by explaining how Aric had chased them out of the castle she threw back her head and laughed.

"And to think he was once under secretary to the Council," she said, wiping her eyes. "But you children have been brave and resourceful indeed. You should be proud."

"But we haven't *done* anything," said Janie. She had come to her purpose: This woman would make a powerful ally. "If you could find some way to get word of this to the Council—"

"We will talk of that later," said the woman, with a faint smile. "Meanwhile, I promised you something to break your fast. Name what it pleases you to eat and you shall have it."

"Uh—cornflakes?" hazarded Janie.

"Cornflakes. I do not know this confection."

"It isn't a—well, what would you suggest?"

After some deliberation the woman scooped up a

handful of water; as the droplets fell, she made passes over them with her staff. And so, out of air and water she created a meal for them, and if it was not exactly the sort of meal they were used to eating, it had at least the attraction of novelty.

There was pigeon pie, minced beef in milk, new bread with butter and cheese, and a salad of wild herbs. These Janie and Claudia ate. There was also venison paste, salted herring, and lampreys in gelatin. These they declined. Dessert consisted of figs and raisins.

"And now," said the woman when they had eaten all they could, "to locate this intrepid sister and brother of yours before moonset."

"*Can* you find them? How?"

The woman silenced Janie with a gesture. Murmuring words of enchantment, she touched the head of her staff to the water in the fountain, and before Janie's and Claudia's astonished eyes appeared an image, shimmering and faint but perfectly recognizable, of Alys and Charles. Alys and Charles were standing in a tangle of hydrangea bushes. The odd thing was, the hydrangea bushes looked just like the hydrangea bushes which grew behind the fountain. . . .

Janie turned an instant before the bushes parted and Alys stepped out.

She had her dagger drawn. Her face was tired and set, but her eyes never wavered from the sorceress. And, as the moon emerged from behind a cloud and shone down on her, it seemed that there was something else about her, something *different*, that brought Janie and Claudia to their feet. The sorceress stood also, swiftly, towering over them all. Her staff was in her hand, and leveled. Moonlight glanced off the gannelin dagger.

Janie's nerves thrilled with alarm.

"No—wait—" she gasped, scarcely knowing which one she was speaking to.

There was a further moment of tension, and then the spell broke. The sorceress lowered her staff. The moon went back behind a cloud. And Alys looked like Alys again.

Janie's immediate reaction, after relief, was familiar annoyance. Alys was her old self again, all right. Trust her to wave a dagger at the only friend they had in the Wildworld.

"This woman," she said aloud, "has just saved our lives."

Alys had the grace to look abashed, and when the sorceress invited her and Charles to sit and tell their stories, she obeyed.

"I finally had the Dirdreth guide us toward the castle in hopes that you had decided to come here," Alys concluded.

Janie nodded. "We did," she said, and explained what had happened to them.

Alys listened intently, but still seemed slightly uncertain and off balance. When the story was finished, she took a deep breath and raised her blue-gray eyes to the sorceress.

"I'm sorry," she said quietly. "I can see now you don't mean us any harm. But I have to ask you—as Janie did— if you mean us any *good*. Will you take a message from us to the Weerul Council?"

The woman smiled. "Now that we are all together I may speak freely. And the answer to your question is no."

There was a murmur of dismay.

The woman shook her head indulgently at them. "Even if I would consider such a thing, there is no need," she said gently. "You children had a mission to find and free the Mirror Mistress, did you not?"

"Yes, but—"

"Then you need search no further. Your quest is done." Standing, she smiled down on them.

"I am Morgana."

For the second time that night Janie was speechless. So were the others.

"So you see," the woman continued gently, "the only job of the Council now will be to punish Cadal Forge—if, indeed, there is anything of him left to punish when I am through."

"But we . . . but you . . . but—*how?*" Janie sputtered.

"How did I gain my freedom?" The woman's smile became grim. "One of Forge's lackeys was stupid enough to visit me with a staff in her hand." The sorceress lifted the silvery staff so that light ran up and down its length. "She dared approach me with it. That was a mistake." With a shrug, she added, "Now I must take the time to prepare myself before confronting Cadal Forge."

"I think he's gone to Weerien to get Thia Pendriel."

"He has returned this night, or so said the careless witch from whom I took this staff. That reminds me: You must keep out of his way, for I cannot protect five at once."

Claudia had something on her mind. "The vixen," she said. "She never came back. What happened to her?"

"I—do not know. I have not seen my faithful friend in this world. Perhaps . . . perhaps she has escaped to the woods." Turning away, with slightly bowed head, she added in a low voice: "I fear for her."

Then she straightened. "But that is my concern, children. As is Cadal Forge. You have listened to his counsels, and have given me much valuable information, and for that I thank you. I assure you it will not be forgotten. But your business here is ended, and you must escape before moonrise."

"But Morgana—er, madam—my lady!" said Alys. "Can you really deal with Cadal Forge alone?"

The sorceress looked at her enigmatically with eyes like dark sapphires. "Have no fear," she said, simply. "But I do not know how long it will take, and you must not come through the mirrors again until I return. Things may become a bit—frenetic—on this side for a while. Promise me."

They promised as she escorted them to the conservatory. The sky was beginning to lighten with the first rays of dawn.

"Good-bye," they all said, and Claudia added, "I hope we see you again."

"Good-bye," said the sorceress, "and you may rely upon it."

When Dr. Hodges-Bradley saw Claudia, she screamed.

They had bicycled home in the pale gray stillness just before sunrise to find that the worst had happened: Their mother, hearing Claudia's shutter banging in the wind, had gone into her room and discovered the doll in her bed. Five minutes later, on finding that she had pillows for older children, she had called the police. And the police had remembered Alys.

"The thing with the banner was bad enough," her mother said to Alys in a tremulous voice. "Climbing up on that clocktower where you could have fallen and broken your neck. But this! The police say that what happened at that house last week and Loara High School last night was real vandalism. And taking your little sister with you! How *could* you do it!"

It seemed that that very night person or persons unknown had thrown buckets of blue and silver paint—the Villa Park High School colors—on the windows of classrooms at their rival school, Loara. And nothing Alys said would convince their parents they had not been involved.

Charles was the only one who persisted in trying to tell the truth. He stopped when Mr. Hodges-Bradley threw the amulet he'd been proffering as evidence into the wastebasket, with the comment that if Charles was trying to be funny he was failing with a vengeance, and that if he was trying to convince them he was crazy he was coming dangerously close to succeeding.

"It's just as well," said Janie, when they had finally been sent to the bathroom to clean up, grounded indefinitely with no TV privileges and no allowance. "If we keep on explaining, sooner or later they're going to think about *drugs*, and then we'll be grounded forever."

"Detentions," Charles mused in funereal tones. Although there was no concrete evidence to link them with the vandalism, in the eyes of the school it was sure to be an open-and-shut case. "Extra laps in gym. Hours of study hall."

"But we did it," said Alys. The transition from the very real terror and danger of the Wildworld to the hysteria in this world had made her a little dizzy. It was the Wildworld that was beginning to seem delusional. "We found Morgana and we helped her. How can you worry about detentions when life as we know it has just been saved?"

"You've never been in Wizinski's study hall," said Charles quietly, and he disappeared into the bathroom.

Downstairs, Claudia secretly fished the discarded amulet out of the wastebasket. She wanted to keep it as a memento.

chapter 16

ELWYN SILVERHAIR

It was December 20, the day before the winter solstice, the second to the last day before Christmas vacation, and Claudia was waiting for school to start. In the four days since Sunday the Wildworld had faded to a sort of feverish dream, and all her thoughts now turned to Christmas. Last year she had been too old to believe in Santa Claus, but by this year she had seen enough to wonder if there wasn't something to the story after all.

Because of her age Claudia had gotten off easier than the other three, and she felt a twinge of guilt as she thought of them spending their afternoons scraping all that paint off the Loara windows. But she felt a worse twinge when she considered what she might find in her stocking on Christmas morning. She was possessed by a deep and pervasive fear that it would be filled with ashes.

"But I am *not* a bad little girl," she said to Kirsten Spiegel, and Kirsten nodded agreeably.

The subject of stockings was of much interest to second-graders. They sat at recess and compared them as to the size. Everyone felt sorry for Amanda Butler because in her family the stockings used had to be real socks, socks the children actually wore.

"And I'm the youngest, so I always get cheated," she said this morning to Kirsten and Claudia. "Look." She pulled off her small blue anklet to show them.

"My brother," said Amanda as Claudia peered solemnly into the sock, "wears a size twelve E shoe. His socks are *enormous.*"

"Well, sure they are," said Kirsten. "He's about eight feet tall, too. Bigger people have bigger feet."

"But is that really *fair?* Is it my fault I'm little?"

Just then the bell rang, and Amanda snatched back her sock and hopped into class. Claudia trailed slowly behind. Something was bothering her; something at the back of her mind was trying to get forward.

Claudia's reading group, the Early Birds, always had a spelling test first thing on Thursdays. Today's was the last spelling test before Christmas. But Claudia found she could think of nothing but feet.

"*Get,*" Mrs. McGiffen dictated from the front of the room. "Please *get* me a present. *Get.*"

Feet, wrote Claudia on her paper. Then she erased the first letter and changed it so that it read G*eet.*

"*Bed,*" dictated Mrs. McGiffen. "Go to *bed* so Santa Clause will come. *Bed.*"

Beet, wrote Claudia. No, that was wrong. She changed

it to *Beedt* and felt better. Why couldn't she stop thinking about feet?

And then, all at once, she knew why, and the anxious tugging feeling became a feeling of disbelief, and then one of horror.

Claudia could not spell another single word on the test, but she hardly noticed. There was a knot in her stomach making her sick. As the spelling papers were handed in, she felt the knot draw tighter until it made her stiff all over. And then she knew what she had to do.

She looked at the clock. Eight o'clock plus five, ten, fifteen, twenty. It was eight-twenty.

She raised her hand to go to the bathroom.

"But you were just outside," said Mrs. McGiffen.

Claudia said nothing, and Mrs. McGiffen sighed and gave her permission.

The corridor outside Room 5 was empty. Her footsteps echoed as she went down the hallway by the third-graders' rooms. She reached the bathroom, passed it without a glance, and crossed in front of the principal's office. No one came out to stop her or say "Where are you going, little girl?" She walked past the kindergartners' playground. Behind the chain-link fence the swings moved slightly in the wind. Claudia walked out through the parking lot to the sidewalk, and then she had left school.

Ashes in my stocking, she thought, and her eyes blurred, but she kept walking.

Far away a dog barked, a horn honked. Up close the world was strange and quiet, like the times when her mother took her out of school for a dentist's appointment. But this time she was not with her mother. She was a truant.

The junior high school was on the same street as her school. Some boys doing laps on the other side of the fence looked at her.

Janie and Charles were in that school somewhere, but this was far too serious to be fixed by Charles or Janie. She had to find Alys.

The two blocks to the high school were the longest blocks Claudia had ever walked. A man watering his lawn stared at her. A dog followed her. Everyone in the world knew she had left school in the middle of spelling.

Claudia knew where the high school gym was. She had taken swimming lessons in the pool there last summer. Still, it was hard to go inside now. High-school girls had to put on special clothes for PE. The locker room might be full of naked girls. But Mother had said, after looking at Alys's midterm report card, that Alys must be spending all day in the gym; so Alys *had* to be inside.

The gym smelled like old sneakers. Rows of metal lockers stared menacingly at Claudia, but there was no one to be seen.

"Hey, who are you?"

A girl with long braids was poking her head out of an office door. The girl looked about Alys's age, but she wore a beautiful silver whistle around her neck.

Claudia backed away. "I—I'm Claudia Hodges-Bradley," she whispered. "I'm looking for Alys."

"Alys Hodges-Bradley? But she's not here now. I think she has Blanchard for geometry this period."

Claudia didn't know what Blanchard for geometry meant.

"Look, I'll show you. See that quonset hut? Well, that's where Blanchard teaches your sister geometry. Okay?"

The door of the quonset hut was open, and if she leaned over the steps Claudia could see the floor inside. She saw rows of desks filled with big students. Alys was one of them.

Claudia whispered, "Alys."

The boy nearest the door looked at Claudia in surprise.

"Alys. Alys," Claudia whispered more loudly.

The boy poked the girl next to him, who prodded the girl next to her, who whispered to Alys.

Alys looked around and saw Claudia.

Her mouth fell open and she dropped her pencil. She glared at Claudia and made a furious go-away motion.

Claudia whispered, "Alys!"

By this time all the students near the door were laughing. Alys sat very stiffly at her desk, eyes straight ahead, refusing to notice. But just then the teacher heard the commotion and came over and looked down at Claudia.

"I think, Ms. Hodges-Bradley," he said, "that you had better step outside and see what this young lady wants."

Flushing deep red, Alys picked up her backpack. Once outside she snatched Claudia out of sight under the stairs.

"Why aren't you in school?" she hissed.

Claudia swallowed miserably. "It's about the magic."

"What? What magic?"

"You know. The vixen. The Wildworld."

"Claudia, you left school to come talk to me about the Wildworld? Now? *Why?*"

"We've got to go back there."

Alys's anger was turning to bewilderment. "But that's all over, Claude."

Claudia shook her head.

"What do you mean? Stop shaking your head and talk!"

"We—we have to go find Morgana."

"Claudia . . . Claudia, have you gone nuts? We *found* Morgana. We met her. She gave you breakfast, remember?"

Claudia shook her head.

"*Stop doing that.*"

"It wasn't Morgana."

A pause.

"What makes you think it wasn't Morgana?"

"Her feet."

Another pause.

"Claudia, I'm only going to ask you this one more time—"

"Alys," said Claudia desperately, "her feet were too big. Remember when we saw the footprints in the secret room? And they were so little? But the lady we met was as tall as Daddy. How could she have feet that small?"

There was a long, long silence. Slowly Alys's expression changed and she sank down to sit on the ground. "No. Oh, no. This isn't possible."

"Don't you believe me?"

Alys squeezed her eyes shut. "Yes," she said at last, very softly. "Yes, I'm afraid I do believe you." She opened her eyes and Claudia saw they were dark with despair. "But, oh, Claudia, what can we do? It's too *late*—"

She jumped to her feet and turned away. Then, very slowly, as if fighting against resistance, her hand moved to her pocket. Claudia saw it come out clenched around something in waxed paper, something small and silvery white. Just as slowly the hand unclenched and Alys stood with bent head, gazing down at what she held. She stood this way for several moments, and then she turned back.

"Alys . . ."

"It's all right," said Alys briefly. Then: "Oh, Claude, don't look that way. It was just a shock, is all. Come on."

"Where are we going?"

"To get Charles and Janie out of school. Tomorrow is the solstice. We've got to do something fast."

Charles and Janie were astonished and puzzled to see Alys appear in the seventh-grade art classroom with a note which said they both had an emergency orthodontist appointment. They were astonished and delighted to be taken out of school at this hour, and they were astonished and alarmed to see Claudia lurking by the gate when they got out.

"Leave your bikes here," said Alys. "We have to talk."

"So," said Alys as they rounded the corner onto their street. "So. Any ideas as to who it actually was?"

"Yes," said Janie. "Thia Pendriel. She would have known all about us from Cadal Forge and Aric." Janie was amazingly calm about the whole thing. The others were numb.

"And you told her everything."

"Yes, and so would you have. She saved our lives."

"That's what I don't get," mumbled Charles. "Why would she do that? And why let us come back here?"

"Because she's *smart*," said Janie. "She got all the information she wanted, everything Aric couldn't torture out of you three, and she didn't even need to use force. She found out that we were only kids, that nobody believed us, that we had no way to fight her. Why not let us come back? After all,"—chillingly—"we'll still be here when she comes through on the solstice. She's smart," said Janie again, sounding almost admiring.

"We have to figure out what we're going to do," said Alys. "I have an idea," she added, when no one spoke.

"Tell it."

Alys told it.

Charles struck his forehead with his hand. "Oh, no. Oh, you've got to be kidding. Please say you're kidding."

"It's the only chance we have left."

"But you *met* her. She's bats, cuckoo, a total space cadet."

"She's one of the Quislais. She has power."

Charles laughed maniacally.

"Stop it. Listen, Charles. We'll lure her over here and trap her with a thornbranch. Remember, the vixen said you could trap a Quislai by tangling a thornbranch in her hair? Then we'll make her help us. Maybe she knows a way to get word to the Council. Or maybe she can help us free Morgana."

"Wait a minute. How're we going to lure her?"

Everyone looked at him.

"Oh, no. No. I won't."

"She liked you," said Alys. "She kissed you good-bye when we left. She told you that if you wanted to see her again you just had to call for her."

"No. I refuse. Absolutely not . . ."

By quarter to eleven Alys had begun to worry about Charles getting back.

She was tired of kneeling by the conservatory mirror

with the thornbranch Claudia had stolen from a neighbor's rosebush in her hand. And she was heartsick about the serpent and Arien Edgewater. Now that Thia Pendriel knew the part they had played, what might she do in revenge? And the moon would set at 10:59 A.M., and where on earth was Charles?

At 10:58 Charles came through the mirror at a dead run.

"Did you—"

"Yes!"

Elwyn came after him, on tiptoe, and Alys pounced. There was a flurry of action and two figures fell heavily to the floor.

"Got you!" cried Alys. The thornbranch was firmly wound in Elwyn's waterfall of silver hair.

Elwyn turned to peer at the thing that was holding her, met Alys's eyes, blinked in perplexity, then frowned. Her breast began to heave with agitation and her cheeks, half-veiled by tumbled hair, flushed pink.

"Why, you—you—" Alys braced herself. "You *naughty!*" cried Elwyn, clearing employing the strongest form of abuse she knew. "I am *vexed* with you!"

"Aw, Elwyn," said Charles. "Give us a chance to explain."

"No more explaining," said Alys. The battle-madness was still singing in her veins. "Now we are going to *demand.*"

"Let me go, you naughty . . . you bad, naughty—"

"Be quiet!" said Alys, thumping her fist on the floor. Then she glanced sharply at the mirror. "Charles, can they—"

"See through? I don't know. I couldn't, but I wouldn't take any chances."

"Right. We'll frog-march her to the nursery."

The frog-marching proved unnecessary, as Elwyn had to follow whoever was holding the branch, so Alys was spared having to admit she didn't actually know what it was. It had just sounded good. She calmed down on the way up and resolved to treat Elwyn firmly but kindly.

Elwyn sank to the nursery floor with tears in her blue eyes. "You are a wicked boy," she said to Charles, "and I am grievously sorry I let you kiss me."

"Charles?" said Janie.

"Oh, shut up and get on with it."

"Elwyn, we're sorry for having tricked you. But you have to understand that this is an emergency." Alys leaned forward and spoke slowly and distinctly, as if to a small child who was also deaf and mentally disabled. "Our . . . world . . . is . . . going . . . to . . . be . . . destroyed . . . tomorrow. If . . . you . . . help . . . us . . . save . . . it . . . we . . . will . . . let . . . you . . . go."

"You . . . hurt . . . my . . . head," replied Elwyn.

A muscle twitched in Alys's jaw.

"I told you," said Charles.

"Please," begged Alys, switching tactics abruptly. "Don't you care at all? Unless you help us we are going to *die*. Do you understand 'die'?"

"No," said Elwyn simply.

Alys, with a terrible chill, felt that without in the least intending to she had at last put her finger on the heart of Elwyn's problem. A whole universe of philosophic thoughts crashed through her mind at once. How could someone who could not die or be hurt understand fear or pain? No wonder Elwyn could be so heartless without being deliberately cruel. She never had to fear the consequences of anything, because to her there were no consequences. Perhaps that was why she remained a child. . . . Perhaps you need to face death in order to mature . . . to take on responsibility. . . .

A great part of her mind wanted to stay and wrestle with these questions before she forgot them. Another part snapped, "Get on with it." Alys, being mortal, made the only decision she could.

"Whether you understand or not," she said levelly, "you are going to help us. Because we're going to keep you here until you do. We won't ever let you go."

Elwyn clapped her hands in exasperation. "I do not wish to stay here and you have hurt my head. If you are not careful I will become very angry."

"And do what, call us names? We've got you."

"Er—Alys—" said Janie.

"Not now, Janie. You see, Elwyn? You're trapped here."

"Alys."

"Hush, Janie. Look, Elwyn, just agree to help us, and afterward you can go home. Come on. Do it. Say yes."

"Oh, I am angry now. I am incensed."

"So spit. I am never going to let go of this branch—"

"Alys, I think there's something you're forgetting."

"—until you give in. All right, Janie, what am I forgetting?"

"Sky-bolts," said Janie, and there was an explosion of light against the far wall, and a crash like thunder.

Alys whirled. The wall now bore a smoldering black spot three feet in diameter. "Elwyn! What—"

Something whizzed by her head and struck the ceiling, shaking the house on its foundations.

"Stop it! Stop it!"

Whiz BANG! Whiz BANG! Whiz BANG!

Alys, appalled, realized that Elwyn was aiming to kill.

WHIZBANG! BANG-BANG-BANG!

Claudia shrieked, caught in a maelstrom of flying glass and wood as the window exploded. The room was thick with smoke and lit almost continuously by flashes like lightning. The air stank of ozone.

KA-WHOMP.

Alys felt as if the top of her head had been blown off. She reeled backward, her hair snagging painfully on a nail in the wall, and slid to the ground. She was clutching a now light and unresisting thornbranch.

"She's getting away!" Charles darted out of the room. Tearing free of the nail, Alys ran after him. They skidded, steadied, and careered into the next room just in time to see an orange-red silhouette disappear in the mirror.

"After her!" cried Alys, but Charles held her back.

"You'll never catch up," he said. "And besides, Cadal Forge is there. I saw him. He's got a whole crowd with him."

Alys sagged. With glazed eyes she stared at the thornbranch in her hand. There was a goodly amount of silver hair hanging from it.

"How could she free herself like that?" asked Janie quietly, from behind them.

"I don't think she did it. I think I pulled the branch free when I fell."

"Yes, I saw that. I believe this is yours." Janie held out a strand of Alys's hair she had collected from the nail.

Claudia groped her way down the hall, which was now billowing with smoke. "There's a hole in the wall back there," she said, coughing.

"Several holes," said Janie.

Charles opened a window. "There's a lot of smoke coming out of the nursery, too," he said. "Who do you like better," he added, "Cadal Forge or the police?"

"Is that a hypothetical question?"

"No," said Alys. "I hear sirens."

The sirens swept up to the house.

Alys's hands balled into fists. "I don't care about Cadal Forge," she said. "I don't care what he does to me. When they come in here I'm going to go through a mirror and show them."

"You can't," Janie pointed out, rather calmly. "The moon set twenty minutes ago."

"But Elwyn—"

"She's a Quislai, remember? Like you said, powerful."

Downstairs the front door burst open.

chapter 17

THE SOLSTICE

The last thing Alys said before the police came running up the stairs, followed by the firemen, followed by the paramedics, was, "Let me do the talking."

For some time thereafter all was confusion, and none of them was quite sure whether they were being rescued or arrested. It seemed to be both, for after they were carried willy-nilly down the stairs, they were handcuffed, put in a police car, and driven to the police station of the city of Orange.

Hysteria reigned. Janie shrilled, Charles shouted, and Claudia, gentle Claudia, bit a police officer. Alys, although feeling dazed and desperate, managed to keep her head. She knew perfectly well that without proof it was hopeless to tell their story about the Wildworld again. At the same time it was essential—it was more important than saving themselves—to convince the police that something terribly dangerous was going on at the old house. If the police believed that, and watched over the house on the night of the solstice, they might have some chance against Cadal Forge.

So she told a story which was as close to the truth as she could get without mentioning sorcery. She said that last week a person had lured them into the old house. As for what had happened inside—well, it certainly *sounded* like a drug-induced hallucination, the way she described it. The person had then threatened them to make sure they kept quiet, and made them promise to come back. There were other people in the house, too, she said, all more or less crazy, like the pyromaniac who had set fire to the nursery tonight.

"Sounds like a cult," muttered one of the officers.

The only problem was that the police wanted names and descriptions of these crazed, drug-dealing cultists. And when Alys couldn't give these, the entire story was seriously weakened.

"I don't believe this cock-and-bull about a mysterious white-haired stranger setting fire to that house today," said the detective in charge of them. "I think you know perfectly well who did it and you're lying to protect them. I think you're probably part of this gang you described. In fact, I'm not sure you didn't set the fire yourselves."

But there was the evidence of the thornbranch—none of the children had hair that color. And the police, despite a search of the house, the grounds, and the children, could not find so much as a burnt-out match to explain how the fire had started. So they were forced to release them. However, it was made excruciatingly clear that if

they ever went near Morgana's house again, or were ever
caught playing with fire, or made any kind of trouble for
the rest of their lives, they would be busted.

Worst of all, it was obvious that although the police
had searched the house, they did not intend to keep it
under surveillance round-the-clock. They certainly
weren't going to stake it out at midnight tomorrow.

There was more hysteria in the car as their parents
drove them home. Alys, her eyes swollen almost shut
with crying, finally put her hands over her ears to block
out her mother's pleas to "just tell us the names of the
cultists."

When the moon next rose, it would be the solstice
moon.

They all cried themselves to sleep.

They were kept home from school the next day, and
spent it in Claudia's playroom—the one with the bars on
the window. Their parents stayed home from work to
watch them. It was nearly unbearable to huddle near the
window with those pale, haggard faces on the other side
of the room.

"What do we do now?" whispered Charles.

"Do?" said Janie.

"We . . . we have to do something. Can't we—can't
we—"

"What?"

Charles shrugged, defeated.

Feeling stupefied, they stared out the window.

At last Claudia said, "Maybe the police will come tonight after all."

"Not unless they have a reason," said Charles. "And

they won't . . . Wait a minute." A light had come into his eyes. "What if—what if we made an anonymous phone call tonight? Told them that—oh, the house was burning down or something. That would get them over there, all right."

All this time Alys had not said a word, but she was not despairing or panicking; she was thinking. Now she slowly closed one hand until the nails bit into her palm, and struck the table a blow that shook the lamp.

"Alys? Is that what we're going to do?"

"No," said Alys. One word, like the beat of a drum.

"Then, what?"

"We are going to burn the house down ourselves."

Claudia shrank back against Charles.

"Alys . . . ?"

"I am not crazy, Charles. I'm serious."

Charles and Janie exchanged an involuntary glance, and then both of them looked quickly toward their parents, who were fortunately still out of earshot.

"Listen to me," said Alys. "It's the only thing we can do that will be of any use. If we set that house on fire just at moonrise, the place will be crawling with police and firefighters by the time the moon enters its quarter and Cadal Forge comes through. Maybe they *can* do something against the Society. And if not—well, I wonder if even sorcerei can step into the middle of a fire and live."

Charles felt cold, but at the same time he was overcome by a sort of horrible fascination.

"It . . . just . . . might . . . work," said Janie.

Everyone considered.

Everyone looked at everyone else.

Everyone let out a long breath and slowly nodded.

"We're going to jail," Charles whispered then.

"I know."

"And—we might be killed. It isn't going to be easy to set a fire that size and get away."

"I think Claudia should be out of it," said Janie.

Claudia didn't even blink. "If you're in it, I'm in it."

"We need gasoline," said Alys. "We'll siphon some out of the cars before we go tonight. And we need a fuse."

A bitter smile touched Charles's lips. "The police accused us of playing with firecrackers. I'll give them firecrackers. I've got some Tijuana *speciales* under my bed."

"The kind that blow your hand off?"

"Oh, Janie. We're probably going to get our heads blown off doing this. What's a hand more or less?"

At quarter to twelve that night they were sitting in the dry brush on the hill by Morgana's house waiting for the moon to rise, just as they had the night they made the amulet. They all wore the amulet at their necks now, as a sort of symbol.

It had been ridiculously easy to climb out their windows and leave the house. Their parents were exhausted after a long day of watching them.

Alys and Charles made precise adjustments in the positioning of the gasoline cans and wads of paper, while Claudia watched with enormous eyes. Only Janie did not participate. She was sitting, chin in hands, gazing unwaveringly at the distant hills where the moon would soon appear. Her face was set and unhappy, but behind the unmoving exterior her brain was running like the insides of a precision watch—which is to say, she thought, in circles.

Janie was a perfectionist. She found the idea of burning down Fell Andred distasteful and untidy. It wasn't the elegant solution. And so even as a silver haze heralded the coming of moonrise she searched frantically for another answer.

The elegant solution, she thought, was to do what they had set out to do in the beginning, to find Morgana. Sherlock Holmes or even Hercule Poirot would have been able to deduce exactly where the sorceress was without ever leaving his armchair. But then, their brains weren't half-asleep.

For that was how Janie felt, as if for weeks she'd been wandering around half-conscious, unable to see the larger perspective. It was because she'd been so afraid of sorcery in the beginning, terrified of the kind of magic she'd heard about in fairy tales, where things happened at random, without rhyme or reason, uncontrollable, unpredictable.

But Weerul magic wasn't like that. The Wildworld sorcery obeyed rules, even if the rules were strange and fantastic. It had a beautiful order all its own . . . and Janie ought to be able to understand it.

Staring at the sliver of white which appeared at the top of the foothills, she put her fists to her temples and tried to *think*.

So many things about Fell Andred had bothered her, so many little things didn't seem to fit—but she couldn't quite make sense of them, and there was so little time. Disjointed fragments of thought rushed past her. The night they'd made the amulet, when they had found that no mirror could be moved from the house. The night she had gone through the double mirrors to rescue the others from Aric. The fight with Elwyn—

Oh, it was no good! With a sharp sound of frustration she shook her head, wishing wildly, illogically, that she were a sorceress like Thia Pendriel. Morgana was somewhere in the castle, Janie felt sure of that, and if they could only work the proper spell they could simply *look* through the mirrors and find her. That is, they could find her as long as . . .

A long, wondering breath escaped Janie's lips, and as the full moon separated itself from the hill it shone upon her transfigured face.

That was it. That was the answer.

Alys was at the door, gasoline can in hand.

"Alys, Charles, put those down."

"What?"

"You're not going to need them."

"What?"

"I know where Morgana is."

Suddenly she felt as light as air. She got up and walked, or floated, to the house, passing Alys and Charles and not looking back to see if they were following her. She knew they were.

"Janie, what are you saying? Answer me, blast it! Where are you going?"

Janie swept through the living room, drawing the others behind her as a comet draws its tail of fire. She led them to the east wing, to the second floor, to Morgana's bedchamber, and she pointed to the smaller of the two large mirrors in the alcove.

"That one, I think."

"Janie, are you crazy? You went through that mirror yourself!"

"So I did," said Janie, smiling, as she gently lifted the mirror away from the wall. Carrying it before her like a shield she walked back into the corridor.

"Where are you *going?*"

With her immediate family skidding behind her, Janie entered the barren nursery.

Alys was frustrated, bewildered, and furious. "But there isn't even a mirror . . . in here. . . ." Her voice trailed off as Janie hung the mirror on the nail which had caught her hair yesterday.

"There is now," said Janie, simply, and stepped through.

There was an instant when all three of the others stood frozen; then, with one accord, they leapt forward to follow, as if released by a spring.

They were so quick, in fact, that they were in time to witness Morgana's first reaction.

"You fools!" she cried, aiming a blow at Janie, which, had it connected, would have laid her rescuer out flat on the floor. "You dolts! You incompetent, beetle-brained numbskulls, is this the best you could do?" She was no taller than Janie, and her gray eyes flashed fire.

"W-we did our best," gasped Alys, thunderstruck.

"Your best!"

"I . . . we thought you'd be grateful—"

"Grateful? Grateful? Do you realize the mirrors will open on the Stillworld in fifty-seven minutes? What in the name of Beldar makes you think I can save you under such outrageous conditions?"

"Possibly," said a dry little voice near the floor, "the fact that they have it on very good authority that you are the best."

"Oh, you're safe!" cried Claudia, stumbling forward.

"There will be time for this later," said the vixen, struggling in Claudia's embrace. "But for now I strongly suggest that you stop ranting, Morgana, and go through that mirror. Why? Because someone is coming up the hallway. Make that several someones."

"You talk too much," snarled Morgana, and then the door shattered and Cadal Forge stepped over the rubble and into the room. He saw Morgana and he saw the mirror and then Alys witnessed the most terrifying thing she had seen in her life. Cadal Forge *focused*. His head whipped back toward Morgana and in his crystal gray eyes there was no longer any trace of abstracted brooding. The entire force of his tremendous will was focused on *now*. Alys reeled.

Morgana, shouting something, dodged into the mirror. But before anyone else could move, the midnight-gowned Thia Pendriel swept forward and touched the mirror with her Silver Staff, and it became transparent, showing Morgana's retreating figure. In a twinkling the tall sorceress turned and snatched Claudia up in her arms. With a quick gesture she tore the amulet from Claudia's throat and tossed it through the bars of the window.

"Now," said Cadal Forge quietly. "To the great hall."

"Claudia!" screamed Alys.

Charles, although he was having strange and inexplicable visions of himself running down Center Street to hide in their garage, joined Alys in following the sorcerei. To his infinite disgust, Janie did not, but vaulted through the mirror after the vixen.

Janie was aware of Charles's scathing look as she passed into the human world. She ignored it and scampered after the sorceress.

"You couldn't even be bothered to bring my staff," said Morgana bitingly as she grabbed something from beside the bedroom fireplace.

Janie, nonplussed, said, "I thought it was a poker."

In Morgana's hands the black, rusty length of metal which Janie had used to beat Aric turned liquid gold, and shivers of light rippled down its length.

"My instruments!" Scarcely seeming to touch the ground Morgana ran to the cellar and down the stairs.

"Take this, and this, and this." She thrust bottles into Janie's hands and scanned the shelves for others.

Janie stared at her. She was thinking that no one could have been more unlike Thia Pendriel. The true Mirror Mistress was as small as a child and her hair fell in a dark cloud to her shoulders. She wore a plain amber-colored robe, gathered at the waist with a wide jeweled belt. At her throat was a heavy gold necklace whose center was a pouch of green silk.

"What are you going to do?" asked Janie.

"Close the mirrors, of course!"

"With the others still in the Wildworld?"

Morgana stopped dead at the sound of Janie's matter-of-fact question. "What?" She looked around the work-room as if expecting to see the other children. "You mean to say they didn't follow?"

Janie told what had happened to Claudia.

"And Alys will never leave her," she finished. "And neither will Charles—I think."

There was a drawn-out moment of tension while the sorceress turned to the vixen and stared at her, eye-to-eye, seeming to have some unspoken conversation.

"Damnation!" cried Morgana at last, throwing up her hands. "I may be half Quislai but I'm not indestructible! Did you *see* how many of them there were?"

The vixen's whiskers quivered. "I always thought," she replied coldly, "that the other half was human."

There was another pause, and then suddenly Morgana was moving again, pulling other bottles from the shelves, her small hands darting with an almost savage deftness as she mixed ingredients.

"Here!" She dashed the mixture into a clean yellow cloth, twisted it, and thrust it into Janie's hands. "The vixen will tell you what to do with this. I'm going to need all the help I can get."

"I thought you were the best," said Janie mildly.

The woman threw her a glance that would have frozen flame in the heart of Hades. "Human infant," she said between her teeth, "our enemies have had three hundred years to prepare themselves for this moment. I have had three minutes. In addition to which I am half a millennium out of practice. I never asked to be the greatest sorceress since Darion Beldar. Now get out of my way, or finish life as a pile of cinders."

Janie obeyed, and she was gone.

"You need a censer for that," said the vixen briskly. "Don't ask why. There is one on that lower shelf."

Janie scrambled among the dusty instruments. Her fingers longed for the lightning deftness of Morgana's.

"What's in the cloth?"

"Incendiary powder. Scatter it to scatter your enemies. Morgana mixes a particularly virulent variety. Unfortunately it must be prepared in small amounts and she had time to make but a little."

Janie found the censer, an ornate gold vessel with holes on all sides, something like a tea strainer hung from chains. "Is there more to the spell than what she did? Because I saw the ingredients and the proportions. And I wonder what would happen if you added just a pinch of phoenix feathers. . . ."

chapter 18

THE GOLD STAFF

Alys and Charles stumbled desperately after the sorcerei to the west wing. No one took any notice of them, except one sorcerer who glanced at Charles in absent contempt and with a casual gesture sent him sprawling.

"Now I'm mad," muttered Charles, picking himself up and wiping blood from his nose. "Now I'm incensed."

"We can't let them have Claudia!" panted Alys.

Just then she reached the second-floor gallery above the great hall, and halted in shock. There had been half a dozen strange sorcerei with Cadal Forge. But in the hall below were easily three dozen more, and every one of them held a staff. The Society had gathered.

An atmosphere of mounting expectation pervaded the enormous room, but no one seemed either anxious or hurried. The sorcerei were tall, with proud faces and elegant, disciplined bodies. Power, and knowledge of power, showed in their every movement. They wore rich robes of many colors: cerulian blue and mandrake green, purple, dove gray, and russet. All eyes were turned on Cadal Forge, who effortlessly dominated this august group by his very presence.

The master sorcerer in his plain soldier's clothes stood near the dais, arms folded, staff in one hand. But despite the apparent ease of his manner Alys could see that he was still *focused*, like a sleeper at last fully awakened.

Suddenly a murmur swelled in the crowd, as the great dais mirror shivered into color. The next moment Morgana herself stood on the platform, her hands empty, tightly clasped.

Her eyes swept the formidable crowd of sorcerei, and when they reached Cadal Forge he made her a very slight bow, as if to say "Voilà." When she located Thia Pendriel, her other great enemy, the councillor expressionlessly lifted Claudia into sight. Morgana's eyes narrowed and her mouth went grim. She turned back toward Cadal Forge, drawing breath, but, unexpectedly, she addressed the room as a whole.

"Members of the Society for a New Order in a New World," she said, and then paused before continuing weightily and softly, "you are being used. This man"—she gestured toward Cadal Forge without looking at him— "has told you that he wants to restore the Golden Age of Findahl, to establish an order where each of you can rule without the interference of the Council. He lies. He cares nothing about a new order. He'd just as soon see every one of you dead—including you, Aric Carpalith. All he wants is the slaughter of the Stillfolk. He wants to wallow in the blood of his personal enemies, and when that is accomplished, *believe me*, the rest of you can go and hang yourselves."

Morgana was a compelling speaker, and when she finished the room was charged with tension. But Cadal Forge still stood at his ease, and when the eyes of the Society turned to him he unfolded his arms, made a small gesture, and smiled.

"I think she's inviting you to leave," he said dryly, and the tension was broken by laughter. But the master sorcerer held up his hand for quiet. "My friends," he said, "by all means leave. Yes, leave—if you do not wish to hold your own land, unquestioned, untaxed, far away from the danger of Chaotic Zones. Leave if you relish the Council forever looking over your shoulder. Leave if you do not want to see a new world, perfect, there for the taking, inhabited only by those barbarians who unlawfully drove us out." He paused, looking at them. "What? Not one of you going?" Then to Morgana: "Stand aside."

Morgana's shoulders sagged, and she turned slowly back toward the mirror. "Cadal, I—*told you I couldn't allow you to do this!*" She whirled back on the last words, and in her hands was the Gold Staff, dazzlingly bright. Out of the head of the staff shot a golden ball which plummeted to the ground, only to erupt upward as a tree of living crystals which grew with lightning speed. Needle-sharp branches burst out in all directions, transfixing sorcerei on every side.

As quickly as that the battle was joined.

Cadal Forge reacted almost instantly, striking the floor a blow with his own staff that opened a fissure beneath the tree, and it shattered. But to do this he had to turn his back on Morgana. Her staff jerked back.

"Hold your hand, Mirror Mistress." The melodious voice of Thia Pendriel rang out in the great hall. The councillor stood directly below Alys. With one hand she held Claudia, who was limp with fear. The other hand pressed the Silver Staff to Claudia's throat.

Morgana's lips drew back from her teeth but she lowered the Gold. A faint tinkling of crystal could be heard as fragments of the tree fell to the ground.

Alys saw Thia Pendriel's jeweled circlet winking far below her, and then her mind simply turned off and her body took control. With a single fluid motion she swung herself over the gallery railing and dropped on the councillor.

The jolt as she hit drove the breath from her body, then she was rolling on the floor, with Claudia in her numbed arms. Thia Pendriel's staff had flown from her hand.

With a terrible, dissonant curse, Cadal Forge threw something toward Alys and Claudia. But at the same time Morgana shrieked something even more high-pitched and hideous, and the bolt from her staff reached them first. It struck the ground in front of them and whizzed around to enscribe a circle from which a racing point of light spiraled up faster than the eye could follow. The spiral became honeycombed, enclosing the children in a glowing lacelike bell jar. Cadal Forge's scarlet sphere impacted with this cage and the lace flooded with red as if absorbing a bucket of blood. The cage then showered sparks from the top and for three heartbeats Alys knew what it was like to be inside a Tower of Gold firecracker.

Then it was gone, but both Thia Pendriel and Cadal Forge had turned their attention back to Morgana, striking simultaneously. The councillor's attack came in the form of a jet stream of silver-blue which Morgana deflected with her staff; the sorcerer's was a bolt of something solid and sharp which grazed Morgana before exploding in the mirror. Before she could recover, they both struck again. The tiny sorceress staggered and fell.

Charles crouched on the gallery, hands white-knuckled against the railing. He was desperately trying to think of something he could do.

A voice spoke by his shoulder. "Here," said Janie. "Take this and use it."

"You! You came back!"

"Of course I came back. I've been whipping up a few spells with the vixen, is all. Take it."

He snatched the object she was offering. "What is it?"

"An incendiary—an explosive powder."

"In a salt shaker?"

"I had to improvise."

Spotting a knot of Cadal Forge's followers below, Janie swung the censer by its chains, releasing a spray of powder.

The effect was spectacular. As each grain was set in motion it exploded into hundreds of tiny pieces, which in turn exploded into thousands of still tinier pieces, and so on. The result was an expanding nimbus of violence.

Even the most expert sorcerei had to turn from the battle to deflect this powder, or else be scorched with myriad painful burns. Joyfully, Charles and Janie raced up and down the gallery, launching hit-and-run attacks on the enemies below.

At first the minor sorcerei had stood back, allowing their leaders to deal with Morgana. But now, the room lit with fitful color as, one by one, the members of the Society entered the battle. Morgana, on her feet again, began to reel under the barrage, unable to defend herself. A shaft of green light opened a cut on her face from cheekbone to ear; a purple bolt, deflected, set the tapestries afire.

Thia Pendriel's staff spat spongy globs of something which smelled like rotten meat. One of these struck Morgana's robe and began to crawl up it. With a gasp that was almost a sob Morgana beat it off, was hit by a lazily rolling scarlet ball as she straightened, and screamed.

Her staff swung in an arc of violence and hit the ground, releasing a flash like electricity. This sped across the floor, ricocheted from the wall, tore back at an angle, and ricocheted again. In its wake it left a line of fire which, as the flash continued its journey, divided the room in a zig-zag pattern. Sorcerei leaped out of the way as the flash passed, then stood trapped between the fiery lines. Alys heaved Claudia onto the safety of the turret staircase, looked up, and was shocked to find she shared her refuge with Thia Pendriel. The woman smiled faintly, nudged her aside, and mounted the stairway, leaving Alys gaping.

In the hall, the flash went rocketing on and the lines glowed more brightly than ever. As it struck the wall for the last time, completing the pattern, the ground began to shake. Out of the lines welled molten lava. Cracks splintered up the walls where the bars of fire touched them, and lava spewed out of these clefts, faster and faster. Morgana paused in her renewed attack on Cadal Forge to look at her handiwork in alarm.

"This is out of control," she breathed. "Children, fly!"

Hearing this, seeing the rising waves of molten rock which rolled slowly across the floor, setting fire to whatever they touched, Alys gripped Claudia under the arms and dragged her up the stairs toward Charles and Janie.

"Up!" she cried as she reached them. Claudia no longer had her amulet and they could not leave the Wildworld without her. There was nowhere to go but up the turret stairway.

In the hall bedlam had broken out. Screams and roars of pain, shouting, spells, and curses swelled into an indistinguishable babble. The three of them carried Claudia higher and higher, to the third-floor level. They reached it just as Cadal Forge succeeded in breaking through the lines of fire. The sorcerei surged past him in pursuit of Morgana, who had taken to the stairs herself.

In an instant Morgana was beside Alys, throwing open the trap door in the turret's roof.

"Climb!"

Lifting Claudia through, the others scrambled up.

"This is my house—and doors, at least, will obey my will," said Morgana, shutting the door, and bringing her staff down hard on it.

"Not if they fall to pieces before your spell is done," said Thia Pendriel, appearing out of the shadows. The Silver Staff spat a burst of fire even as Morgana's Gold began to trace the outlines of the door. There was a silver light and a searing heat. The extent of Morgana's weariness was made clear when, instead of protecting the children by sorcery, she simply shoved them out of the way.

And, through the hole in the floor of the turret, the sorcerei arrived.

"Behind me," said Morgana quietly, and they obeyed.

The tide of the battle had turned. Morgana, bleeding from a dozen wounds, faced the staffs of two dozen murderous sorcerei. Cadal Forge, at the front, slowly lifted the Red Staff to the level of her heart.

"Surrender," he said, simply.

The Mirror Mistress was silent.

The sorcerer spoke softly. "I did not kill you before," he said, "and I would not kill you even now. Submit to me, yield me your staff, and you may live—you may even go from here in peace. Otherwise . . ."

He made a small, eloquent gesture.

"Face me alone," the tiny sorceress burst out hoarsely. "Fight me without that herd of slavering sheep at your back, and if I am defeated you may take my staff in honor."

"I will accept that challenge." Thia Pendriel stepped away from the others. "Our quarrel is an old one, Renegade, and I welcome the chance to settle it."

"Pendriel, you're a fool," said Morgana. Her hands had clenched convulsively on her staff and her voice shook despite her control. "What would you do with the Gold, after all these years? And where can you go with it, now you have openly betrayed the Council?"

The tall sorceress smiled enigmatically.

"To the Stillworld? Would you really enjoy lording it over a land of wretched, short-lived slaves? Or perhaps you, too, have some other purpose. . . ."

"Enough," said Cadal Forge. "There will be no single combat and no more debate. You have wasted too much of my time already. Look at me, Morgana. The Red is your death."

To Alys's unspeakable horror the griffin's head on his staff came alive. The eyes rolled, the mouth gaped open with a lionlike roar, and out poured a cloud of red vapor which swept toward Morgana against the wind. As if at a signal all the other sorcerei struck at once. There was a light like a rainbow, and Alys saw the floor rush up toward her.

She regained her senses to feel a stinging pain in her arm. At her back the turret wall was in ruins. In front Morgana had fallen with the Gold Staff under her body, and Cadal Forge stood above her, preparing to finish it.

Out of the griffin's mouth, from which thornbranches had once sprung to trap a Quislai, long, fibrous tendrils now emerged. They wrapped themselves around Morgana's body almost caressingly—and then they began to tighten.

Alys watched, unable to look away. The whole scene was like a nightmare, and it reminded her vividly of another nightmare, when she had lain helpless with fear and watched a friend face death alone. But now, somehow, she was not lying still. She was on her feet, dizzy, with the gannelin dagger in her hand.

No one bothered to cry a warning to Cadal Forge as she sprang—what could a mere human do to a master sorcerer? But the sorcerer was not Alys's target. One sweep of her arm brought the dagger across the writhing tendrils, cutting through them as if they were cobwebs. Morgana drew a tortured breath as they fell from her throat, and lay still.

Alys turned to meet the crystal gray eyes of Cadal

Forge. Once before she had met that searing gaze in a mirror and had panicked. Now, she kept her grip on the dagger and stuck at him with all her force.

And then the Red Staff itself lifted high, whistling down to meet the gannelin knife. The dagger shivered into a thousand fragments and the shock sent the hilt flying from Alys's hand and Alys herself staggering backward. She stumbled as a piece of rubble turned beneath her foot. For a moment she swayed on the edge of the turret, trying to regain her balance, then the stone gave way beneath her and she fell.

chapter 19

HEART OF VALOR

Alys's scream was snatched from her lips by the shrieking air as she fell. The full moon lit the ground below in terrifying detail. And then suddenly some great shape surged between her and the ground and she shut her eyes and hit it, and it dropped with her, so that they skimmed Fell Andred's outer wall before rising steeply.

She opened her eyes and gasped, clutching wildly. The castle was far below, a toy, and she was circling and wheeling up somewhere near the stars, and the huge head which looked over its shoulder at her inquiringly . . . was the head of a snake.

A voice by her ear said, "My lady Alys—"

Streaking through the air beside her was the serpent, her own serpent, its blue and coral body supported by six pairs of velvety blue wings. Dumbfounded, she looked back and forth from it to the monstrous creature which bore her up.

"I told you I was only an infant of my kind," the serpent reminded her gently. "The others are larger."

The others were larger. For the first time Alys realized that the night was filled with giant wheeling shapes, crimson and black in the moonlight, even now beginning to dive toward the castle.

"Your wings—" she shouted into the roar of the wind, as the creature she was riding swooped downward.

"The Eldreth's pool!" the serpent shouted back, plummeting beside her. "Be ready to jump off, my lady!"

The turret seemed suddenly to blossom below her, and the next thing she knew she had leaped off her seat and Charles and Janie were beating her on the back in a frenzy of joy.

Another kind of frenzy had broken out among the sorcerei. As the great serpents, the guardians of the Weerul Council, descended, the braver of the Society launched many-hued flares of sorcerous power at them. But the enormous creatures seemed impervious to such attack. They continued to dive, striking like the great snakes they were, until the turret shook under the blows, and the sorcerei trampled one another as they fled. It was a rout.

Alys laughed and cried and clapped her hands. Morgana, guarded by two serpents the size of eagles, slowly sat up.

"The day that I should accept my life from the Council!" she commented, white-lipped, to no one in particular.

Above them, a sweet wild voice rang out. " 'Way for

the emissary of the Council! Clear the ground for the Council's elect!"

Charles, who had been dancing about in exuberance, now turned his face up in shock. "It's Elwyn!"

"Elwyn?"

The silverhaired girl was riding on the back of the largest serpent. As it dived she leapt off and dropped lightly to the ground.

"Oh, you're dirty," she said, and without waiting for an answer she darted off again, adding sky-bolts to the fray.

By now the turret was rocking violently under the blows from the serpents and blasts from the sorcerei. Suddenly, in a thunder of falling stone, one entire side gave way, exposing the spiral stairway, now broken in many places, and the second floor of the turret.

Alys and Janie staggered on the lip of the ruins, trying to keep their balance on ground that buckled and split like a living thing.

"We can't stay here," gasped Alys. But Janie clutched her, staring down into the tower.

"Look," she said. "Down there—the mirror!"

On the second floor of the turret something was happening to the mirror set in the wall. It started with the familiar, ever-changing pattern in blue and green, but then the patterns began to shift more and more quickly, and the dancing colors grew brighter, until they dazzled the eyes. And then, with a sound both deceptively soft and terrifyingly loud, a sound of such low pitch that it was almost beyond human hearing, blinding blue-white light shot out from the glass. All over the castle it was the same, as if each mirror were a searchlight which had suddenly been switched on, and the radiant beams streamed from every room, through every doorway and window and crack in the masonry.

The full power of the last great Passage was unleashed and the square bulk of Fell Andred shone like a star.

Every face turned upward to look at the full moon.

"It's entered its quarter," whispered Alys. "The mirrors are open." But even as she spoke she saw the silhouette of a soldierly figure jump from the steps directly into the rectangle of light.

Alys gasped. "Oh, *no*. Morgana—they're using the Passage! They're going into *our* world!"

The Mirror Mistress was already on her feet.

"Quickly, follow me!" Somehow, between crawling and falling, they all got down the ruined stairs. Elwyn appeared beside them as they plunged into the radiance of the mirror.

After the violence and grandeur of the Wildworld, it was a terrible shock to step into a perfectly whole turret in this world. But the blue light streaming from the mirrors was nearly as bright, and from somewhere below in the house came shouts and explosions. It seemed that every member of the Society still able to move had fled through the mirrors to escape the great serpents.

"What can we do?" cried Alys to Morgana as they ran down the turrent stairs.

"You can keep out of it," the sorceress returned rapidly. "You can't leave the house—I've already activated the wards around it to keep *them* from escaping—but you can hide. For pity's sake give that little one a rest!"

Alys was all but carrying Claudia by now. She looked frantically around the living room and her gaze fell on the small alcove beside the mirror.

"Stay here," she said, setting Claudia in it. From somewhere the vixen came running to jump into Claudia's lap.

"I will watch over her," she said, her proud yellow eyes meeting Alys's grimly. "You go and help my mistress. She needs it."

Morgana was in the kitchen, pausing long enough to drive a sorcerer into the mirror with golden lightning bolts before turning hurriedly to the cellar steps.

"Once we have forced them all back into the Wildworld I must close the mirrors for good and all," she said. "It's the only way to end this mischief. Elwyn, make yourself useful!"

Janie followed her down the steps. Elwyn, with a merry laugh, began to seek out and chase sorcerei. And Alys and Charles were left to themselves in the west wing.

They made an attempt themselves at chasing the enemy. But although many of the Society had lost their staffs, and many were panicked and disoriented, when they saw it was only unarmed children who pursued them, they fought.

"A ruse," said Charles, snapping his fingers suddenly as Alys jerked him for the second time out of the path of orange death. "Charles, m'boy, you're brilliant." He pulled a firecracker out of his bulging pockets, lit it in the flames the orange death had kindled in the wall, and threw it at the sorcerer who had attacked him. To the man the subsequent explosion of sparks meant only one thing, and he fled through a mirror to escape what he supposed to be incendiary powder.

"Wheeeee—yah!" shouted Charles, racing about looking for more sorcerei. "Here, take some!" he yelled to Alys.

"All right, but try to pick on the ones without staffs!" Alys shouted as he rocketed away. She saw an empty-handed sorceress peering around a door and hastily lit a firecracker.

The sorceress took to her heels, and Alys gave chase, lobbing the firecracker at her retreating back. But to her surprise the woman turned, apparently driven to fury by this assault. Her green eyes blazed at Alys, who took a hurried step backward, realizing that even an unarmed sorceress was far too dangerous for a human to take on alone.

But she was not alone. Something like the lash of a blue and coral whip whisked past her ear at the sorceress. With a cry, the woman fled through the mirror.

Alys, who had sat down without meaning to when the serpent flashed by, straightened up and rubbed her ankle. It circled gracefully back to her and lighted on her knee to gaze at her.

"Thank you." She felt strangely shy.

"Lady, if I were to spend my life trying to repay you I could not do it. That pool of healing restored what I thought lost forever . . . my wings."

"I nearly killed you in the marsh. . . ."

"And risked your own life to save me after. Arien Edgewater told me. She told me also of the flower—it is a very great honor to be given that. And she sent her greetings by me to Alys Friend of the Eldreth." With a last loving coil about her wrist, it flew into the mirror to pursue the sorceress.

A voice behind her bawled, "I got five, how many did you get? And Alys, guess what?" Charles added, grinning wickedly as he reached her. "I chased Aric through the cellar mirror. Get it? The cellar. Where the Groundsler is." He beat his thighs in an excess of delight. "Hey— what's wrong?"

"Nothing," said Alys, blotting her eyes and getting up. "Come on, let's go to the east wing."

They jogged back through the kitchen, into the living room—and stopped, frozen.

Across the length of the room, beside the blazing shield of light that was the mirror, Alys could just make out the faint outlines of Claudia and the vixen. But much nearer, tracing glowing sorcerous patterns on the door which led to the outside world, was Cadal Forge.

He had his staff. And he was by no means either panicked or disoriented.

Neither did serpents bother him—at least not serpents of the size that could come through the mirrors. As Alys stood paralyzed, one of Morgana's eagle-sized guardians soared over her head at him, and the master sorcerer drove it with scarlet fireballs step by step into the huge mirror near the stairway.

The maneuver took him within arm's reach of Claudia. A surge of adrenaline flooded Alys from head to foot. She lunged forward—and a hand gripped her shoulder, small but firm and steady. Shakily, she stepped aside to let Morgana pass and closed ranks with Elwyn and Janie and Charles behind the sorceress.

The door on the outside wall still glowed, but Cadal Forge could not reach it to complete the spell which would pierce the wards. The Mirror Mistress barred his way.

In her left hand she held a white cloth, to which the remains of a golden powder still clung. The head of her staff, dusted with this powder, was tipped with a ghostly flame.

"Cadal," she said. In the eldritch light streaming out of the mirror her face looked pale and tired, and her voice was drained of feeling. "Go back," she said. "You can't get out. It's over."

Cadal Forge seemed tired, too, but he smiled. "Morgana," he said, very gently, "it is just beginning."

Over his face once again came the look of abstraction, of dreamlike reflection, but now it was mingled with an expression almost of tenderness. And . . . of deep joy.

"I had hoped to go somewhere else to do this—perhaps Roma. Perhaps Firenze," he said, musingly.

"No." Morgana shook her head. "While I live, while Fell Andred stands, neither door nor portal shall open for you. You shall not leave this house—"

"But there is no need." With a low laugh, his eyes shining darkly, the sorcerer reached into the folds of his tunic and drew out something which glittered like red ice.

Morgana let out her breath softly. "One of the *bas imdril* . . ."

"Heart of Valor."

"Cadal, you *are* mad. The peril of touching such a thing . . ."

"Touching it?" The sorcerer had been holding up the Gem to admire it, his smile as tender as a lover's. Now he looked sharply at Morgana. "Touch it? I *created* it. Yes, I did. . . ." His gaze drifted back to the jewel again. "Cast into the very wellspring of Chaos, I strove, and conquered, and found this at my feet. Forgotten too long, Unmade even, it has now returned. See it shimmer?"

"Cadal . . ."

"The moment I saw it I knew my lifework, my purpose. And the Society?" Laughter spilled from his lips. "Oh, those fools. I needed them, you see, to escape the Council. And to deal with you, my old friend. . . . So I thought. But now—let them go hang themselves." He caressed the Gem, and deep within it a red light stirred. "You see, I never meant to let them rule at all," he said softly.

"What, then?" breathed Morgana.

The sorcerer did not answer her directly. "You have never seen what I saw in the Well of Chaos," he murmured, gazing into the Gem. "So you cannot imagine. . . . But stay—you can see it now. In here."

He raised his eyes to Morgana. "Do you begin to understand, my dear, old friend? This lovely thing was created from the very horrors of hell. All the power of anarchy is trapped within it. Trapped. Seething. Waiting to be unleashed—"

"No!" cried Morgana.

"—as only I can unleash it."

"Cadal, for the love of God! It means your own death as well—"

"It means all I have ever desired. It is my purpose, to bring an end to a world which should never have begun. Oh, see it! See it shimmer!" He lifted his voice joyfully as the Gem glowed brighter and brighter, casting a crimson light on his transported face. "Heart of Valor, awake! Taken from the realm of Chaos, let Chaos blossom in you once more! Lay waste to all around you. Wreak a desolation which shall slowly consume this world, inescapable, unstoppable, resistless. Still the Stillworld forever!" The red light now surpassed the blue light from the mirror, illuminating every corner of the room.

"Look into the Gem and see it coming!" As the sorcerer held the jewel aloft he saw Claudia for the first time near his feet. "Yes, *you*, little human, daughter of my enemies, *you* look. Gaze into the depths of the Gem. Can you see what lies behind the light?"

All this time the vixen had been crouching on the floor like a stone statue of a vixen. But now, as the sorcerer roughly caught Claudia's arm to force her to look into the jewel, she forgot herself, forgot that she was a mere familiar, and that she had no place in the workings of great magic. With one wild snarl of pure animal rage she sprang full in his face, a clawing, biting, scratching whirlwind. And Cadal Forge, used to defending himself against spells and conjurings, was taken completely unawares. Flinging up his hands to ward her off, he reeled backward and lost his balance. With a cry of pure astonishment he tumbled into the mirror.

The jewel, its light dying, skittered by Alys's feet. Quicker than thought, Morgana sprang forward and clapped her flame-tipped staff to the rectangle of blue, and the flame on the staff and the light of the mirror came together in the greatest of all implosions. Unbelievable, searing radiance flooded the room, causing them all to gasp and shield their eyes. And then with a sound like the crack of a giant whip the mirror shattered, a shattering that was echoed from every other room in the house, in a series of deafening crashes so close upon one another they seemed like one long sustained explosion traveling outward.

When the last echoes were gone Alys slowly opened

her eyes and unstopped her ears. Claudia lay on the floor, dazed but alive. The vixen, every red-gold hair on end, stood beside her snarling. The brilliant white light had died to a sullen violet glow, and now, even as she watched, this glow disappeared like a guttering flame.

The mirrors were closed.

"Look," whispered Charles.

Beneath the network of cracks that covered the surface of the large mirror was the silhouette of a man. Red-orange, against a frozen blue-green background, it might have been a masterful impressionistic painting of a subject in the act of falling. But it was not a portrait.

Cadal Forge had not made it back to the Wildworld.

chapter 20

THE MIRROR
MISTRESS

Morgana stepped back from the mirror, lowering the Gold Staff as if its weight was suddenly too much for her. "Oh, Cadal," she said softly and sadly, eyeing the shadow in the mirror. "Perhaps this will keep you out of trouble." And then, without any fuss, she crumpled to the floor and lay still.

The others were around her in an instant. A moment earlier Alys had had the idea that there was something she ought to do at the back of the room, but there was too much to think about now and Morgana was frighteningly pale. Her face was bluish white under the blood and bruises. Alys and Charles lifted her to a couch and put pillows behind her, and she was as light and fragile as a dry leaf, and so very motionless, and so very cold.

"It's all right," said Alys. "I've had first aid, I know what to do." She spoke around the squeezed feeling in her chest and the hammering of her heart as she searched for a pulse in Morgana's thin wrist.

"Sure," said Charles. He stood a few steps away, opposite Janie, arms folded tightly. Claudia, very pale herself, sat and blinked as if she could not focus her eyes.

Alys's hand shook as she released the tiny sorceress's wrist. "It'll be okay," she said again. "I learned CPR. I can—you can live even if your heart's stopped for—"

Janie bent over and pulled at Claudia. "Come on." Her eyes, meeting Alys's over Claudia's brown head, flickered toward the Gold Staff on the floor. It was black and rusty once more, looking like nothing so much as an old fireplace poker.

Alys stared at it for two heartbeats. Two of her own heartbeats; Morgana had none. Then she nodded at Janie.

"Take her out," she said.

Claudia, understanding, began to sob. The vixen ran up to the staff, sniffed it, and backed away, stiff-legged, bristling. Then she began to streak back and forth wildly across the room, cursing Cadal Forge and all sorcerei, the children and all humans, and Elwyn and all Quislais.

"Stop it!" Charles recoiled at the noise, looking frightened. "Alys, why don't you do something? She'll be all right. She's *got* to be all right."

"Don't be a fool, boy." The vixen had come to a ragged halt at last, crouching under the table. But despite the harsh words there was no asperity left in her voice—only pain. "Didn't you see what she did? Closing a Passage— the greatest of Passages—at the very height of its power!

Slamming it shut and locking it tight with the moon still rising! And before that. Taking on the whole Society by herself, *and* a Red Staff, *and* a councillor—and with you to protect as well. Anyone else would have given you up to save your world, but not she. She was a fighter all her life."

Alys flinched at the "was" and flinched, too, remembering that she, Alys, had at one time been willing to give Morgana up to save her world.

Appalled, Charles rounded on Elwyn, who had been hovering at the edge of the group like a luminous dandelion. "You," he said harshly. "With your sky-bolts and your immortality. She's your sister. Can't you do anything?"

Elwyn looked bewildered. She cocked her head to one side and then opened her lips. But it was Alys who spoke and she spoke to Janie.

"Quick," she said, in a voice she herself did not recognize. "Get a glass of water."

Janie didn't turn. "She can't drink. Alys, she's—"

"Get it," whispered Alys.

When Janie came back Alys's hand trembled, clenched around what she had taken from her pocket. She had lost the dagger and she had lost the serpent. She would never see Arien Edgewater again. But as she unwrapped the packet of waxed paper and drew the silver-veined flower out, her hands suddenly steadied. She crushed the flower into the glass and bathed Morgana's pale, still face with water. The scent of Arien Edgewater's pool rose around her, sharply sweet. When she had finished she put the Gold Staff in Morgana's hand, and stepping back, she sank to her knees before the sorceress to wait.

"Please," she said softly to no one at all.

Slowly, one by one, the others knelt around her. Even Elwyn, after an uncertain look at Charles, faltered and joined them. But Morgana's lashes were dark crescents against the lifeless pallor of her face, and neither breath nor heartbeat stirred her body.

The vixen bowed her red-gold head and whimpered.

And then something magic happened.

Almost as if awakened by the vixen's cry, a tiny glimmer of gold rippled down the rusty staff. As they watched, unbreathing, another joined it, and another. Like sparks on a wire, like shining beads of molten gold, the glimmers raced and multiplied until the entire staff was alive with them, swarming, throwing a pattern of light on Morgana's face.

In that shimmer of gold they saw the deathly pallor retreat from the sorceress's cheeks. The shadows around her eyes faded. And then her lips parted and her breast rose and fell with the intake of breath.

They were still on their knees, encircling her, when the sorceress opened her eyes. She looked at them in surprise, then quickly took a deep breath, one hand fluttering to her face. Her astonished gaze fell on the glass, which still held a few drops of water and the remains of the flower.

"Malthrum!" she cried. "But which of you could possibly—" And then for some reason she looked at Alys. "Never mind," she said, sinking back, still looking at her. Then, quietly: "I thank you."

Alys swallowed and nodded, her cheeks hot. And the others, as if suddenly released from paralysis, broke into joyous hysteria.

The vixen leapt onto Morgana's lap, and then off again, rolling on the floor like a puppy. Charles embraced Janie, who was wiping her cheeks with a look of mild surprise, and then—to be quite fair—he embraced Elwyn, too. Everyone was laughing and crying and shouting excitedly until Morgana's voice cut through the pandemonium.

"Hold, hold!" she said, struggling to a sitting position. "I don't mean to sound ungrateful—I am not—but would you all kindly hold your peace? Thank you. Before we all give way, there is something vitally important that we must do. We must search the house for any sorcerei who remain."

Everyone looked involuntarily over his or her shoulder.

"Yes," said Morgana. "My wards won't hold much longer, if indeed they have held this long. And now that the mirrors are closed there's no sending anyone back to Findahl. Leave this little one—Claudia, is it?—with me, and I'll see she's all right."

The serpent, thought Alys, as everyone moved to obey Morgana. She had been right in her suspicions; now the Passage was closed for good, and it was gone forever. She told herself it was for the best, that a Feathered Serpent could no more live on earth than she could live in the Wildworld. But in the midst of telling herself this she remembered its bright black eyes and felt the weight of its tail coiled trustingly around her wrist, and her throat ached.

She met Charles and Janie back in the living room. Morgana had taken Claudia and the water glass into the kitchen.

"Did you see any sorcerei?"

"Not a sign of one. How about you, Janie?"

"Well, there certainly are none in this house. May I ask if you expect to find them under the rug?"

"No." Alys straightened. "I was just looking—don't you remember that red thingummy Cadal Forge had? The jewel."

"It went into the mirror with him."

"No. It went by me. It ought to be here—"

At that moment she was interrupted by a siren.

The three of them looked at each other and stiffened.

"Sounds like a whole convention," said Charles as another siren joined it, and another.

"Sounds like they're coming *here*," said Janie.

Charles ran to the front of the house and returned, breathless, to peer through the living room curtains.

"I think they're surrounding the house," he shouted grimly, over the noise.

"Let them come around back like anyone else," said Morgana's voice from behind them. "The wards have fallen and it will be some time before I can raise them again." Although the sorceress supported herself against the kitchen doorframe, both she and Claudia looked greatly recovered. "That front door hasn't been opened in over a century," she added, slowly crossing the room and easing herself into a large chair by the hearth.

From the back drive brilliant lights pierced the curtains, shifting and moving, and then fixing. Suddenly all the sirens stopped. The dead silence was eerie.

"After all we've been through—oh, I can't believe this," said Alys. "First the Society, now the police. It's like a joke."

"I see five cars out there," said Charles, letting the

curtains fall back into place, "and those rifles are no joke."

Alys helplessly turned to look at the small sorceress. "Morgana," she said, swallowing, "we've run into the police before. I don't know how to explain. . . . It's all gotten so *complicated*—"

"Ah," said Morgana. "I see. Let me think."

Just then a voice from outside crackled over a loudspeaker, causing all four Hodges-Bradleys to jump. "Alys—Charles—Janie—oh, Claudia," said the voice. "Darlings, if you can hear me, please, please, give yourselves up."

"Mom!" said Alys. She, along with the others, had started toward the door, only to stop short in dismay and frustration. "Morgana . . ." said Alys, gasping.

"All right," said Morgana. "Come here and listen."

Outside, the full moon had reached its apex, shining down on the fortresslike old house on the hill. It shone serenely on the five police cars fanned out on the old house's back drive, it reflected off the metalwork of the car doors behind which ten officers alertly crouched, and it picked out glints of silver on the barrels of the rifles those officers held aimed toward Fell Andred. It just touched the edge of the loudspeaker that Dr. Hodges-Bradley held as she knelt, weeping, with the police lieutenant in charge, and it added its force to the searchlights turned on Fell Andred's back door until the doorway was lit brighter than day. And, as that door slowly opened, it illuminated something else.

Behind the lieutenant ten rifles snapped into position, five searchlights swung, and fifteen officers stiffened, ready for anything. And then, from all around, there was a universal murmur, like a hushed, long-drawn-out "Whaaat?" and rifles were slowly lowered as the men and women who held them craned their necks to get a better look.

In the doorway, in the moonlight, gazing fearlessly into the searchlights with wide-open eyes, was a young girl. She wore a flowing gown of irridescent colors, and her face was impossibly, inhumanly beautiful. Her hair, which fell unbound in waves to her knees, was palest silver.

Ten rifles dangled from unheeding hands as officer after officer slowly rose to stare in wonder.

Elwyn Silverhair looked around at them and smiled.

"You," she said, pointing. "And you, and you. Come inside with me. You have been granted an audience."

"First," said Morgana to the lieutenant and Dr. and Mr. Hodges-Bradley, "I must ask you to smell this leaf."

"What?" began the lieutenant, but then he broke off and pulled his head back sharply, blinking and wrinkling his nose.

"Unpleasant, I'm afraid," agreed Morgana. "But it will make our conversation so much easier." The sorceress sat erect in her thronelike chair by the fireplace, with the richly woven cloak Alys had fetched from upstairs about her shoulders and the Gold Staff across her knees. The leaf which Janie had brought at her direction from the cellar was crushed between her outstretched fingers.

"You see," she continued calmly, as Dr. and Mr. Hodges-Bradley also began to gasp and blink, almost losing their frantic grip on their children, "I am a sorceress, and this is my house. And these four young people, whom apparently you have been harassing, are under my protection."

The lieutenant, spluttering angrily, was rubbing at his eyes with his sleeve. "What the—" All at once he broke off and lowered his arm. On his face fury gave way to surprise and then to mild embarrassment. Alys looked at her parents and saw that it was the same with them. All three of the human adults were glancing about apologetically as if they had suddenly awakened from a nap during dinner.

"I—I'm sorry." The lieutenant looked down at the vixen, who sat regarding him with eyes like narrow slits of gold, then turned back to Morgana. "You were saying?"

"I was saying that far from being criminals, these children have done both me and your city a great service. They have risked their lives to rid this world of a rather serious menace."

"Menace, ma'am?" said the lieutenant.

"A sorcerer who forced his way into this world in order to destroy it." Morgana explained briefly about Cadal Forge and the Society. "But have no fear, he has been vanquished and is now an extremely handsome specimen of modern art. I plan to turn him sideways and hang him over the sofa."

Everyone followed her gesture to the great mirror behind her, and Dr. Hodges-Bradley tightened her grip on Claudia.

"Oh," she said, quietly. "How horrible."

Morgana turned back sharply with narrowed eyes. Then she dropped her gaze. "Well, yes, perhaps it is," she murmured tiredly. Alys was suddenly aware of the effort it was costing the little sorceress to keep erect.

"In any case," she resumed, looking up again, "you can see that your concern over our welfare is needless, lieutenant. I think you may go back to your officers."

"Ma'am, I hardly know what to say to them."

Morgana smiled. "Have no fear. You see, that was Worldleaf I gave you to smell. A breath or two of its essence and you are able to perceive the truth in its purest form, despite the clouds of old prejudices. However, the effects don't last. Truth in its purest form is lost and only vague impressions remain. In a short time, you will forget what I have said, and all that will remain is the conviction that these four children are somehow heroes. You will tell your officers a perfectly plausible story which you have invented in your own mind."

"I see, ma'am." The lieutenant hesitated. "And, ah, just when do you expect it to wear off?"

"I should say about—now," said Morgana, watching him.

The change that came over the three adults' faces now was similar to the one they had undergone before. They blinked and looked briefly disoriented. Then they recovered.

"And so, if I have explained everything satisfactorily—"

"Oh—yes, ma'am. I just—now that's odd—" The lieutenant was gazing at his blank notepad in perplexity. "I wonder why I—that is, I'm glad to have this thing cleared up at last. We'll keep an eye out for intruders like the one you mentioned. I remember the description—I think. . . ." Frowning and muttering to himself, he made his way to the door.

"For my part, I'd like to thank you for taking care of

the children," said Mr. Hodges-Bradley to Morgana. "Under the circumstances you've told us about, which—which were certainly very—" He broke off, looking doubtful. "Under those circumstances, I should say—"

"We'd better bring the car up from the bottom of the drive," interrupted Dr. Hodges-Bradley. "Claudia shouldn't walk so far in the cold." The door shut behind them, and Morgana settled back.

"Honesty is occasionally the best policy," she said, yawning. And then she added, "By the Black Staff of Beldar, I am tired. If I can find a usable bed in what's left of my house I intend to collapse on it. And Elwyn, if you disturb me before dawn, I *promise*, I will turn you into a train of thought, and lose you."

And, without another word, she went up the stairs.

"Well!" said Alys.

"Good-night," said Elwyn.

It was astonishing how tired they were suddenly. All night they had been whipped to a fever pitch of excitement, and now, with the police gone, and Morgana gone, and nothing more to face, reaction set in. Alys all at once felt incredibly numb and stupid.

"Bed," she muttered dimly as they stumbled mechanically down the drive. And then:

"Oh, blast!" she groaned, and stopped. "Wait a minute," she mumbled. "I've got to go back. I was looking for that red gem of Cadal Forge's—"

Janie caught her by the arm. "Don't bother."

"Eh?"

"It's long gone."

As they all looked at her in surprise she pulled something out of her jacket pocket. "I found this by the conservatory door. Outside the house."

In her hand was a scrap of midnight blue and silver.

Alys started. "Thia Pendriel! You mean she's *out*? She's loose? And you didn't tell Morgana?"

"Morgana," said Janie flatly, "is half-dead already. I think any more of this really would kill her. And, besides, *she* will be miles away by now, with the Gem. She isn't stupid."

"Well . . ." Alys hesitated, her weary brain trying to get hold of this. "Tomorrow morning you come straight back here and tell her. Do you hear me?"

Headlights appeared around a corner and swung toward them, and Janie shielded her purple eyes.

"I'm way ahead of you—as usual," she said.

chapter 21

THE SECRET OF
THE MIRRORS

The next morning everyone but Janie slept late.
The others woke to find she had been gone for hours.
When they went outside the vixen was seated on the
porch.

"You want us to come with you, don't you?" said Claudia happily. The vixen gave them a patient look and
trotted off.

At Morgana's house Janie was seated with the little
sorceress in the kitchen. Morgana wore a clean fawn-
colored robe and she seemed once more in perfect health.
Elwyn, her silver hair bound up in a red scarf, was holding
a feather duster. She was dusting Morgana.

"Janie," said Alys, "did you tell—"

"She has told me everything," said Morgana. "And it made for grim hearing. I blame myself for not watching the Gem more carefully. However, for the moment there's little to do about Thia Pendriel; and I think, all told, last night came off pretty well. Certainly better than I could have expected, as I sat in the nursery watching the solstice moon rise."

"Oh! That reminds me," said Alys. "There are some things I've been wondering about."

"Such as?"

"Well, first of all, how did Janie figure out you were in the nursery—"

"—and second," interrupted Charles, "*where* did Elwyn get those serpents?"

"Oh, I went to Weerien," said Elwyn carelessly. "I really don't know why, I was so very angry with you. Oh, I was exceedingly wroth! You hurt my head, if you remember. And you said you were going to keep me forever, and for a moment I almost believed you. Why, you *frightened* me. It was a wicked thing to do." Her jewellike blue eyes opened wide.

Alys thought that being frightened for once was perhaps the best thing that had ever happened to Elwyn. But she also thought it would be rude to say this, so she held her tongue.

"So I went back to my wood and resolved to think no more about it," Elwyn continued. "But somehow I couldn't stop thinking. It's a sore puzzle to me why not. I pondered and pondered it, trying to decide what to do, and at last, just when my head was about to burst asunder, I had an idea. I thought to myself, Why, this is high politics. It isn't your business at all, and I really don't know what the boy—"

"Charles," said Charles.

"—what the Charles boy expects you to do about it. And then I had a wonderful inspiration, which was to take the problem to the Weerul Council and let it fret them instead."

"But that's exactly what we *begged* you to—"

"And so I hied me as fast as I could to Weerien, to get it off my mind," said Elwyn, speaking right through Alys's remark. "And would you believe it, when I got there, the Council wouldn't listen! They thought I was playing a prank! Imagine that! Oh, it was vexing!

"Finally, just when I was about to give up—I'd been thrown out of the Council chambers, you see, and I was wrother than ever—I felt a little brush of wings on my shoulder. I looked and saw a Feathered Serpent, a babe yet, still blue."

"Oh!" said Alys eagerly.

"Yes. It had been sadly injured by Cadal Forge, and then put into a pool of marvelous healing or something. The very moment it was healed it wriggled out of the pool and flew straight to Weerien. And that was that, you see. Because one of us the Council could disbelieve, but not both. And, oh! Weren't they upset! They sent a hundred of the guardians back with us to deal with Cadal Forge, and we all flew back to the castle. Serpents fly fast. I like them, don't you?"

"Oh, yes," said Alys.

"But I do *not* like the Council. They were extremely cross and annoyed with me for moving the mirror once

Morgana was in the Wildworld, and the language they used was not at all nice."

"So it *was* you who moved the mirror," said Janie. "I thought it must have been."

"Wait a minute, wait a minute," said Alys. "Elwyn moved the nursery mirror?"

"Of course," said Janie. "She was the only one who could have done it, because it had to be done from this side."

"How do you know?"

"What I don't understand is how I *didn't* know for so long. It was obvious."

"All right, Sherlock, it was obvious," said Charles. "So explain to us morons. I want to hear how you figured out where Morgana was in the first place."

"From the mirrors. That's where we should have started. No, not going through them, Charles, but analyzing them. Let's put it this way: The mirrors in this house are here to travel through, like doors. So, logically, there should be one mirror for each room. Any less would be inconvenient and any more would be redundant. But the nursery didn't have any mirror, and in Morgana's bedroom there were *two*. And on the nursery wall was a bare nail, showing that something had once hung there. Remember, Alys? You caught your hair on it when we fought with Elwyn. Clearly someone had moved a mirror from one room to another. But the vixen said Morgana hadn't touched the mirrors since she gave up practicing magic. When you look at the facts it becomes pathetically obvious."

"You mean when Elwyn moved the nursery mirror to

the bedroom it closed off the Wildworld nursery from this one?"

"Right. Like locking a door."

"But why didn't she just break the mirror? Or throw it out the window?"

"Only Morgana can break the mirrors—right?" Janie looked at the sorceress, who nodded confirmation. "And we tried to take a mirror out of the house that night we made the amulet, remember? We couldn't."

"The mirrors in this house," said Morgana, "are not ordinary objects, but Passages, or potential Passages, to the Wildworld. Furthermore, the mirrors on this side control the mirrors on the other side. If you take a mirror off the nursery wall in this world the Wildworld mirror disappears because the Passage is closed. If you then carry that nursery mirror into the bedroom and hang it on the wall you punch a new Passage through to the Wildworld and a mirror appears on the other side. So when my irresponsible sister did this idiotic thing I suddenly found myself trapped in my own nursery with no mirror, no staff, and no hope of escape."

"That's right," said Elwyn, seemingly not bothered at all by her sister's strictures. "I just let Morgana go through the mirror first, and when she did I took the mirror off the wall as Cadal told me to. He told me to break it, too, but I couldn't, so I just carried it into another room. It was easy."

Charles was intrigued. "So a Passage forms wherever you put a mirror," he said. "What if you put a mirror on the floor and went through?"

"Then you should emerge standing on your head and look extremely ridiculous," said Morgana tartly.

"Anyway," said Alys in the silence which fell after this remark, "I think Morgana is right. We did pretty well, considering. The Society is scattered, Cadal Forge is trapped in the mirror, and Aric's undoubtedly been eaten by now."

"And, seeing that everyone is happy," said Elwyn, "I will take my leave. I am very curious about this Southern-california of yours. I want to visit Holly's Wood."

Charles's mouth drooped a little. "You mean—you're going away?"

"Yes." Elwyn pulled off the scarf and shook out her starlike hair, apparently all the preparation she was going to make. "Good-bye, all of you. Good-bye, boy. You may kiss me, if you like, as a token of my forgiveness."

Charles blushed. "Good-bye," he mumbled, leaning forward to peck the air beside Elwyn's cheek. "Good-bye, and . . . and I forgive you, too."

Elwyn dimpled merrily. "I daresay we'll meet again."

And then she was gone, and the house was a little darker and a little colder for her absence.

"But won't she get hurt?" Charles turned to Morgana in dismay. "I mean, she doesn't know anything about the modern world. Won't she—well, cross against a light and get run over by a Greyhound bus or something?"

Morgana laughed. "More likely, within the hour she'll be playing cruel tricks on some poor unsuspecting human. Never you worry about a Quislai, my lad.

"And now," she added, "to the reason I summoned you this morning. In the past weeks you have worked very hard, and suffered no little, and received nothing in return."

"We saved the world," said Charles softly.

"You saved this world from Cadal Forge. There are many other dangers—equally great—that humans have created for themselves. The story is not all told yet.

"But in any case, I would like to give you a small token of my appreciation.

"You first," she said to Alys. "Come with me." Alys and the others followed her out to the back drive. And there, capering about the garden on dainty hooves, was a milk white colt. It was fine and slender and spirited, with large curious eyes and legs much too long for its body. It took one look at them, tossed its white mane, and with a flip of its tail was galloping off in the opposite direction.

"Wild," said Morgana, shrugging. "Like his mother. Never been touched by human hands. But you ought to be able to catch him eventually if you bring some rope. Every hero should have a horse."

Charles snorted. "But Alys isn't a hero."

"And the colt isn't a horse—yet," said Morgana.

Alys was staring after the rapidly disappearing speck of white, electrified. "Are you serious? I can have him? For me? For my own? Oh, but this is the most *wonderful*—" She stopped, hearing in her mind an echo of Claudia's tremulous voice, "What do you think is the most wonderfulest, specialest, excitingest thing in the world?"

"Oh . . . thank you," she breathed.

"For you," Morgana was saying to Claudia, ignoring Alys's raptures as they returned to the house, "the vixen will visit you at her convenience, and you have my permission to enter this house and visit her until such time as you annoy me beyond the limits of toleration."

"Or prove yourself unworthy of so great an honor,"

amended the vixen coolly, but she did not move away from Claudia's stroking hand.

"For you," said Morgana to Charles, "this." Into his open hand she pressed a little glass box which held a lump of whitish rock.

"Gee, thanks. Uh . . . what is it?"

"Oh, don't you remember?" broke in Alys, repressing a fit of giggles. "What you told Claudia was the most wonderful, special, exciting thing in the world? When she asked us that night we went to see the vixen? Charles, it's—"

"Kryptonite," said Morgana. "Or, to be precise, it is the element krypton; there is no such thing as the other. I advise you not to open the box as krypton is a gas at this temperature."

"Kryptonite." Charles turned the box over. "Well . . . what do you know? How nice."

Alys choked back a laugh. She was still terribly exhilarated. "But what about Janie?" she said. She was rather expecting Morgana to produce the Hope Diamond.

"Oh," said Janie, as everyone looked at her. "Well, actually, as it happens, Morgana is going back into the magic business. Because of Thia Pendriel being loose, and because—well, because she doesn't like being so out of practice. And the fact is she needs an apprentice."

"An . . . apprentice?" said Alys.

"Yes, and I'm it." Unable to help herself, Janie grinned outright. "She says I've got a talent for magic—a sort of flair, you know. The vixen first noticed it when we were mixing up the incendiary powder."

"But—but—can humans do sorcery?" asked Charles.

"You've already done some yourself, if you recall," said

Morgana. "Although, of course, the amulet spell was just child's play—literally. I made it that way. But to answer your question, I don't see why not. The Council wouldn't like it, but then the Council isn't here. And desperate times call for desperate measures."

"You'll be able to do *magic*," said Claudia to Janie admiringly.

"Oh, well." Janie tried to look matter-of-fact and humble, failed dismally, and grinned again. "Of course, I've got to learn the basics first," she added briskly. "Latin and German and Old English for reading Morgana's books. Botany and organic chemistry. Metamorphic petrology . . ."

Charles was horrified. "You *want* to do this?"

"Oh, yes! I've wanted it all my life, without even knowing what it was. Charles, you have no grasp of the tremendous potential involved here, the infinite possibilities, the challenge—"

But Charles had gone back to trying to pry the lid off his box of Kryptonite with his thumbnail.

"Anyway," said Janie, turning to Claudia, "I can do one thing for you right now, if you like. Morgana and I have been discussing it, and we think it's a pity that you and the vixen can't talk while you're outside this house. So we're going to whip up a spell—a really old spell, and a hard one, too—that will allow you to understand her anywhere."

"I'll be able to talk to animals?" Claudia began to stutter in her excitement. "Like—like Doctor Dolittle? You mean I'll be able to t-t-t-talk—"

"*Not* to animals," said Morgana forcefully, pausing by the cellar door. "To the *vixen*. And only to the vixen. We can't have you wandering about holding conversations with every stray mongrel you meet. It's a waste of time and energy and you never know what it might lead to. Do you understand? *Not* to animals. Now, come along, Janie."

Claudia blushed and ducked her head. She hadn't meant to seem greedy. It was enough to be allowed to talk to the vixen, she knew that.

But as the little sorceress and her familiar descended the steps, Janie stopped in the doorway. She turned. Slowly, deliberately, she winked one purple eye at Claudia, and smiled.

"Somehow the idea of Janie and magic together makes me very nervous," said Charles when the doorway was empty.

"She'll be supervised," said Alys vaguely, thinking of her horse. "Morgana won't let her do anything too awful."

"Yeah, but just imagine it. Newts crawling out of the woodwork on junior talent night. Bliss Bascomb getting mange. Hey!" He cheered up suddenly. "Maybe she could hex my geometry teacher."

"Or keep the weather decent for at-home games. Hmmm . . ."

Musing, they drifted to the back door.

"Coming, Claude? We're going home to find some rope."

"I have to stay for the spell," said Claudia, surprised.

"All right."

They went outside. Even in midwinter the California sun was warm and bright, and a little breeze blew across the orange grove, stirring their hair.

Alys gazed down dreamily at Villa Park. "All this," she announced to Charles, "is still here because of us."

"Yeah," said Charles cynically, "but nobody knows it."

"Mom and Dad know. Or anyway they know we did something. And," she added, struck by a sudden thought, "I'm sure they know in the Wildworld."

The more she thought about this the more certain she became. The serpent, her own serpent, had undoubtedly told the story to the Weerul Council, and presently word would get around. Perhaps someone would write a song or story about it.

Yes, or an epic poem in heroic couplets. The tale of Alys the Valiant who, heedless of the danger, had single-handedly led a small band of untried warriors against a master sorcerer. Alys the Stalwart, friend of marsh dwellers and Feathered Serpents, conqueror of Quislais, fearless traverser of the mirrors. And why should the story end there? Someday, perhaps, there would be further tales of Alys the Intrepid and her white steed Winter, champions of justice and defenders of the oppressed. Tales of Alys the Undaunted, the gallant, brave, and resolute . . .

"Hey, Alys," said Charles, "do you think Morgana would let me trade in my Kryptonite for a dirt bike?"

Alys the Heroically Valiant, Conqueror of Thousands, disappeared and all that was left was Alys the Sensible, everybody's big sister and confidante. She sighed and then smiled at Charles.

"I don't see why not," she said. "Anyway, it couldn't hurt to ask."

"I saw an ad for one in the paper the other day, a Kawasaki KX80. Water-cooled motor, front disc brakes,

KYB leading axle front air forks, six-speed transmission . . ."

"Sounds wonderful," said Alys, thinking of her horse.

"Or maybe a Honda XR500 . . . only you need a driver's license for one of those. Hey! Maybe Morgana could get me a driver's license. . . ."

They walked on down the hill.

Inside the house a fly buzzed lazily in the sunshine. Claudia opened a window to let it out. The kitchen was drowsy and warm and still, as if keeping its own secrets.

She sat down to wait for the vixen.